To This Day

Books by the author

The Bridal Canopy

In the Heart of the Seas

Betrothed & Edo and Enam: Two Tales

A Guest for the Night

Twenty-One Stories

Selected Stories of S.Y. Agnon

A Dwelling Place of My People

A Simple Story

Shira

A Book That Was Lost and Other Stories

Agnon's Alef Bet: Poems

Only Yesterday

S.Y. Agnon

TO THIS DAY

TRANSLATED AND WITH AN
INTRODUCTION BY
Hillel Halkin

The Toby Press

To This Day

First English Edition, 2008

The Toby Press LLC
POB 8531, New Milford, CT 06776–8531, USA
& POB 2455, London WIA 5WY, England
www.tobypress.com

Originally published in Hebrew as *Ad Hena* Copyright
© 1952, Schocken Publishing Ltd., Tel Aviv

Translation and Introduction copyright © Hillel Halkin, 2008

Cover art: George Grosz. *Gray Day*. 1921.
Oil on canvas, 115.0 × 80.0 cm. Inv. B97.
Nationalgalerie, Staatliche Museen zu Berlin, Germany
Photo: Joerg P. Anders/Bildarchiv Preussischer
Kulturbesitz/Art Resource, NY

ISBN 978 1 59264 214 4, *hardcover*

A CIP catalogue record for this title is
available from the British Library

Typeset in Garamond by Koren Publishing Services

Printed and bound in the United States

Introduction

Published in 1951, *To This Day*, the slimmest of Shmuel Yosef Agnon's six novels and the last to be translated into English, has also made the least mark in Hebrew. Agnon critics have tended either to ignore it or to dismiss it as an episodically meandering work that ends with a trite attempt at closure.

They are wrong. Agnon, always a great literary trickster who delights in fooling his readers, has this time fooled the critics, too. Not only is *To This Day* as carefully conceived and tightly written (to say nothing of entertaining) as any of his novels, it yields to none in its brilliance and depth. If it appears to meander, this is because the loops in its course deflect our attention from the course itself; if its conclusion strikes us as trite, we have fallen into the trap Agnon set for us. And having said as much, I would suggest that, if you prefer your first encounter with a novel to be a direct one without an introduction getting in the way, you skip the rest of these remarks and return to them after reading *To This Day*.

*

Suppose then that, having read Agnon's novel, you were asked to write a brief summary of it. It might go like this:

The narrator of *To This Day*, a young man in his middle or late twenties with scholarly and literary ambitions, has left his traditionally Orthodox family and native town in Austrian-ruled Galicia in Eastern Europe to settle in Palestine. After spending several years there, he has moved to Berlin—where, at the story's outset, we find him living in a rented room during World War 1. Trapped in Germany by the war, he is, as a citizen of its ally Austria, eligible for military service and required to report regularly to a draft board, which has so far granted him a temporary medical exemption.

The narrator's main preoccupation, however, is finding and keeping a room in a wartime capital suffering from a severe housing shortage. His ordeal begins when he travels to a town outside Berlin at the request of the widow of the deceased scholar Dr. Levi, who wishes to consult with him about her late husband's large library of Judaica. In the course of this trip, he also encounters three other people: the former stage actress and wealthy socialite Brigitta Schimmermann, with whom he appears to have been—perhaps unconsciously—in love before her marriage; his cousin Malka, a Zionist like himself, who cannot understand what made him leave Palestine; and Hanschen Trotzmüller, the shell-shocked son of the landlady of his Berlin boarding house, now recuperating at Brigitta's rural convalescent home for wounded soldiers. Though aphasic and amnesiac, Hanschen, in a prophetic fulfillment of a dream had by his mother, mysteriously follows the narrator back to the boarding house and is reunited with his family and restored to his old room, which the narrator, now left homeless, has been renting.

All this occupies the first half of *To This Day*. Much of the novel's second half describes, in frequently comic terms, the narrator's subsequent wanderings from one rented room to another. Each room has a fatal flaw; each compels him to search for a better one that turns out to be even worse. And meanwhile, as the tide of war turns against Germany, Berlin becomes a nightmare of shortages, ersatz products, refugees, bereaved families, maimed and crippled war casualties, shrill patriotism, nouveau-riche profiteers, and a garishly decadent *après-nous-le-déluge* nightlife of cafés and cabarets. Still, the narrator, who now dreams of returning to Palestine, remains detached from his surroundings. The sufferings of others, despite the concern he expresses for them, do not touch him deeply. When the war ends and he does return to Palestine, arranging for Dr. Levi's books to join him there, he can only think of how lucky he has been to have survived his experience safely. To his mind, the war and all its horrors pale beside his personal good fortune.

*

So much for our summary. From it we can extract a number of motifs that recur throughout the novel. One is the disposition of Dr. Levi's books. Another is the narrator's flirtatious relationship with Brigitta Schimmermann. We might add to this his incessant room hunting; the oppressive atmosphere of wartime Germany; his attitude toward the war as a Jew and a foreigner; his feelings about Zionism and Palestine; his self-centered personality; and his repeated reflections on life's purpose or lack of it. Each of these motifs, moreover, intersects at numerous points with others. The narrator's involvement with the Trotzmüllers, for example, though primarily the story of how he comes to be homeless, also touches on the barbarism of war and the seemingly miraculous chain of circumstances that bring a traumatized soldier home again. Brigitta Schimmermann, for her part, is linked to the war by means of her nursing home; to the books of Dr. Levi, whose residence with its library is not far from her; to the narrator's musings about purpose and causality, since it is through her that he encounters Hanschen, and so on and so forth. Upon closer inspection, *To This Day* resembles an intricately woven spiderweb whose strands crisscross repeatedly.

Scanning this web for its patterns, we might rephrase our summary as follows:

On the eve of World War 1, a young Eastern-European Jew leaves Palestine, to which he has gone to live for Zionist reasons, and moves to Berlin. Although he has presumably done so in the hope of broadening his horizons, all he himself can say is that the "notion" to return to Europe somehow "got into" him. Perhaps he has difficulty acknowledging his guilt at abandoning the Zionist cause; perhaps he cannot admit to himself that he is seeking not only intellectual and cultural adventures, but sexual ones as well, such as his liaison with Lotte Trotzmüller. For all his wit and quickness of mind, he is far from an introspective individual, a point he himself makes more than once, as in the long "shaggy dog" story that he relates to Brigitta Schimmermann, the anti-Freudian moral of which is that it is a waste of time to probe oneself too deeply.

Indeed, no longer the religiously observant Jew he was raised as, yet retaining a strong love and nostalgia for Jewish tradition, the narrator seems to have no real understanding of the battle going on within him between his allegiance to his Jewish faith and identity and his craving for a broader realm of experience. This battle can only be expressed by people and events outside himself—and if one pole of it is represented by the captivatingly worldly Brigitta Schimmermann, the other is associated with Dr. Levi's library, a rare repository of the Jewish past and its wisdom that stands to be lost. Because of their geographical proximity, Brigitta's nursing home and Levi's library exert a joint attraction whose separate pulls the narrator is unable to distinguish. By reading between the lines—and Agnon must *always* be read between the lines if we are to slip through his net rather than be caught in it—it is even possible to conclude, as does the Israeli critic Nitza Ben-Dov in her perceptive study *Agnon's Art of Indirection*, that the narrator's initial journey to Dr. Levi's widow, which sets *To This Day* in motion, is also motivated by his desire to find Brigitta.*

And yet toward Brigitta, the narrator is deeply ambivalent. While drawn to her, he is also scared of her, there being no other explanation for his forgetting to ask her at what restaurant they are to meet after he is overjoyed to run into her in the Leipzig train station and be invited to lunch with her. (The restaurant's turning out to be

---

* Ben-Dov, however, is mistaken in my opinion in treating Brigitta as the epicenter around which the whole of *To This Day* revolves rather than as one of its two antipodes. In doing so, she skews the novel's symbolism and structure.

named "The Lion's Den" is yet another knot in the novel's web,* as is an additional mental slip that occurs at its end, when the narrator repeatedly tries phoning Brigitta at her nursing home only to discover that he has been dialing the wrong number.) In part, he fears the sexual feelings she arouses in him; in part, her German patriotism, whose betrayal of the humane cultural values she espouses is embodied in such details as the toy cannon placed by her on an open volume of a Russian author and pacifist like Tolstoy.

Throughout the novel, eroticism and the violence of war are intertwined in the narrator's mind. Both are depicted as fundamentally German or Gentile traits that spring from a single libidinous source where love and hate, tenderness and cruelty, and sexual and military conquest arise together; both suggest to the narrator, who is a vegetarian, an animality that he associates with the eating of meat and with the butcher shops, besieged by German women brandishing ration books, that line the street below one of the rooms that he rents. The theme of raw meat runs even more strongly through the comic episode of the goose liver given him by his cousin Malka. Intended as an innocent gift, the bloody liver that he can neither enjoy nor get rid of is the perfect symbol of his own repressed sexual and aggressive feelings.

It is significant that, although there are also Jews in *To This Day* who are mindless supporters of the war, the only principled opposition to it apart from the narrator's comes from other Jews—especially from the bibliographer Isaac Mittel, who foresees Germany's defeat

---

* How cunningly this knot is tied is apparent when one considers that the Hebrew for "The Lion's Den," *me'on ha-arayot,* can also be punningly read to mean "the home of forbidden sexual relations." This play on words is of course untranslatable, as is a great deal of Agnon's unique prose—which, an idiosyncratic literary construct based on rabbinic Hebrew and often turning its back on the spoken language of Israel, is in effect an imaginary dialect of its own. In seeking to find a direct English equivalent for it, many of Agnon's translators have ended up with something that is neither Agnon nor English. Here, as in my previous translation of Agnon's novel *A Simple Story,* I have avoided such an approach in favor of an idiomatic English that strives to convey the special flavor of Agnon's style in more roundabout ways. There is, to borrow Nitza Ben-Dov's apt phrase, an "art of indirection" to translating Agnon as well.

at an early stage when the nation is still drunk from its military triumphs and his own son has yet to be killed in battle. As opposed to Jews and learning, Jews and gunpowder, Mittel observes, do not go together. Nor do Jews and the erotic. While several of the female characters in the novel are Jewish, all the women who openly display their sexuality, such as Lotte Trotzmüller, the Trotzmüllers' Aunt Clothilde, or Frau Munkel and her daughter Hedwig, are Gentile. The revulsion they provoke in the narrator, like that provoked by the war, is the age-old revulsion of the Jew for the "goy." It is also, however, a revulsion for the unacknowledged "goy" within himself that has drawn him to Berlin in the first place.

Despite the differences among them, the Jews in *To This Day* fall into two categories, native-born German Jews and East-European Jewish immigrants and refugees, between whom there is tension and mutual scorn as well as a fraternal bond. In this respect, Agnon's novel is sociologically faithful to the times. German Jews tended to look down on the *Ostjuden*, as they called the Yiddish-speaking newcomers from the East, as uncouth, uncivilized, and unscrupulous, while the latter considered the *Yekkes*, as they referred to them, to be Jewishly ignorant, gullible, humorless, and absurdly proud of being German when most Germans did not consider them as such. In the one scene in *To This Day* in which the two parties confront each other, the *Ostjuden* represented by Yudl Bieder and his friends, and the *Yekkes* by the businessman Kitzingen, each amply confirms the prejudices of the other.

The narrator, who numbers both German and East-European Jews among his friends, sees the good and bad side of each group. The character he most admires, Isaac Mittel (whose name means "middle" in German), is in fact a blend of both, a Polish-born Jew who came to Germany at a young age and has lived most of his life there. Mittel combines the *Ostjude*'s Jewish knowledge and ironic perspective with the *Yekke*'s cultivation and probity, and he maintains an intelligently sane point of view throughout the novel. Not even his coolness toward Zionism detracts from the narrator's esteem for him, for it is not the defensively hostile anti-Zionism of the German Jewish patriot but the honest skepticism of a man who wonders how Zionism can succeed, and suspects that Jews are better off as a minority that does not put all its eggs in one basket and has its faults tempered by others.

Mittel's is one of two voices in the book to express such doubts about Zionism. The other belongs to Malka, an intellectually simpler person but one who raises an equally salient question. In inquiring why her cousin has left Palestine after living there for only a few years, she asks how a people like the Jews, who have spent their history wandering from land to land (or from room to room, in the symbolism of *To This Day*), always seeking better opportunities, can ever hope to settle down in one place. Although the narrator, unwilling as usual to contemplate his own behavior, prefers to change the subject, he knows Malka has a point. Having himself chosen homelessness in Berlin over a home in Jaffa that, however now romanticized by him, was indeed pleasant to live in, what can he expect of the Jewish people as a whole?

Berlin and Jaffa are as much opposed in *To This Day* as are Brigitta Schimmermann and Dr. Levi's library. In a sense, these two pairs of opposites are one. Levi's library is out of place in Germany because an increasingly assimilated and intermarried German Jewry has no use for it, just as it has none for the Hebrew books collected by Isaac Mittel, whose own son cannot read them. Only in a Zionist, Hebrew-speaking society, Agnon's novel implies, can Jewish culture find a permanent asylum, so that rescuing Levi's library and returning to Palestine are a single challenge. While the Zionist project may or may not be the only viable option for the Jewish future, it is certainly the only one for the Jewish past.

We can now restate our summary of *To This Day* once again. Set against the background of World War 1 Berlin, Agnon's novel, we might say, is a story about Jewish exile and Jewish home-seeking; about Diasporism and Zionism; about Eros and Thanatos; about Christian civilization and the Jewish critique of it; about chance and causality; about self-knowledge and self-deceit; about a young Eastern-European Jew, a sharp observer of others who is peculiarly blind to his own self, in whom all these elements play out; and about how he finally chooses, after a long period of unconscious struggle, the Jewish and Zionist side of himself.

Indeed, who but a blind man could look back on the events leading up to this denouement as does the narrator? Here is his own summary of them at the novel's end:

> Consider what happened to a man like me. Living in cramped quarters without pleasure or sunlight, he received a letter from Dr. Levi's widow asking to consult with him about her husband's books; traveling to see her, he found her hopelessly ill; returning to Berlin in frustration, he had nowhere to lay his head, his room having been given to another; finding another room that he liked, he was soon driven from it and forced to wander from place to place, from room to room, and from tribulation to tribulation, his worries multiplying without cease. And yet just when it seemed that he could no longer bear one more of them, God had mercy and delivered him and returned him to the Land of Israel. Is not all that seems for the worst, then, really for the best? And the best of all I've saved for last, which is the house this man built in Palestine. Not being one for grand notions, he knows that he built it not for himself but for Dr. Levi's books, which needed a new home.

Although coming from someone who is far from stupid, such a conclusion, at the end of a cataclysmic world war, strikes us as inane, especially since the narrator has told us (a seemingly minor detail when first encountered) that he has read Voltaire's *Candide*, the classic European satire on the belief in a benevolent universe, and is or should be aware that he is echoing its final, mocking lines. In them we find Voltaire's hero, who has wandered the world and witnessed great natural disasters and every kind of human brutality, living with his old love Cunegonda in the pastoral setting to which they have retired. With them is Candide's childhood tutor Dr. Pangloss, Voltaire's caricature of the German philosopher Leibniz, who earlier in the novel has instructed Candide:

It is demonstrable that things cannot be otherwise than as they are; for as all things have been created for some end, they must necessarily be created for the best end. Observe, for instance, that the nose is formed for spectacles, therefore we wear spectacles. The legs are visibly designed for stockings, accordingly we wear stockings…and they who assert that everything is right, do not express themselves correctly; they should say that everything is best.

Now, at the book's end, Pangloss tells Candide:

There is a concatenation of all events in the best of possible worlds; for, in short, had you not been kicked out of a fine castle [in which Candide was raised] for the love of Miss Cunegonda; had you not run the Baron [Cunegonda's brother] through the body; and had you not lost all your sheep [loaded with a fortune in gold], which you brought from the good country of El Dorado, you would not have been here to eat preserved citrons and pistachio nuts.

To which Candide replies laconically, "Excellently observed, but let us cultivate our garden."

Yet while there is a hint of irony in this reply, suggesting that Candide, although too polite to say so, has come to realize how fatuous Pangloss is, no such irony is detectable in the final remarks of the narrator of *To This Day*. What, it seems fair to ask, is Agnon up to?

*

One thing he is *not* up to is identifying unequivocally with these remarks. Indeed, he has already distanced himself from them midway in the novel by introducing the character of the narrator's old friend Shmuel Yosef Bach, who proposes quite a different conception of reality. By means of the scene with Bach, Agnon accomplishes three things. First, by having the narrator tell us (in no other place is this mentioned) that he, too, is named Shmuel Yosef, Shmuel Yosef Agnon the author signals us that we are reading an autobiographical novel.

Secondly, through Bach's informing the narrator of the anti-Semitic atrocities committed by the Russian army and Ukrainian peasantry in Galicia, he makes us aware (here, too, for the only time) that there is a dimension of specific Jewish suffering to the war. And thirdly, by attributing to Bach a philosophy of life diametrically opposed to the narrator's at the novel's end, Agnon alerts us to the fact that the latter's point of view is not necessarily his own.

What is Shmuel Yosef Bach's philosophy? Explicated in a book that he is writing and thinking of calling *On The Repetition of Things*, it is reminiscent of Nietzsche's doctrine of "eternal recurrence." Life, Bach declares, has neither purpose nor direction. Rather, it consists of an endless series of random events that sooner or later (there being only so many possibilities) repeat themselves in what appear to be meaningful patterns—and it is in these imagined patterns that we mistakenly see a guiding hand in the affairs of the world, though in reality they are an illusion, an attempt on our part to impose a cognitive order on sheer chaos.

Ultimately, Shmuel Yosef Bach and Shmuel Yosef the narrator must be thought of as a single person, as is borne out by Bach's background, which is similar to Agnon's own. Whereas Bach's family, we are told, descends from the renowned rabbi Yeshayahu Hurvitz, (d. 1631), Agnon's family claimed as its ancestor the equally renowned Shmuel Idels (d. 1630); whereas the Bachs own a fabrics store, Agnon's parents owned a fur store; whereas Bach's father is an admirer of the medieval poet and biblical commentator Abraham Ibn Ezra, Agnon's father was a devotee of Ibn Ezra's contemporary, the philosopher Maimonides, and so on. In effect, the two Shmuel Yosefs are two sides of the author, with whom they shared a single life from birth until one of them left Galicia for Palestine and the other did not.

*

This happened in 1908. In that year an aspiring Hebrew author named Shmuel Yosef Chachkes, born in 1887 in the town of Buczacz in today's western Ukraine, settled in Palestine's main port city of Jaffa, soon to spawn the new Jewish neighborhood of Tel Aviv. Chachkes did not keep his family name for long. That same year one of his first published stories appeared in a Hebrew periodical. It was called *Agunot*, "Abandoned Wives," and its author signed it, in a play on its title, "S.Y. Agnon." Gradually, the pseudonym adhered to him.

Agnon spent four years in Palestine, partly in Jaffa and partly in Jerusalem, working in various secretarial and editorial capacities while continuing to publish and to acquire a reputation as a rising star in Hebrew literature, especially after the serialization in 1911–1912 of his novella *And The Crooked Shall Be Made Straight*, a folkloristic tale set in mid-19th-century Galicia. Nevertheless, in the autumn of 1912 he sailed back to Europe. This was not unusual for a Zionist settler of that period. Palestine was small and provincial, its climate difficult, its opportunities few, its Jewish population of 75,000 growing at a snail's pace; for every new arrival there was someone else, so it seemed, who departed. Berlin was a great cosmopolitan city and a center of Jewish and Hebrew culture. Agnon put Zionist and other sentiments aside (his close friend and the man he most looked up to, the older and more famous Hebrew writer Yosef Haim Brenner, had implored him to stay in Palestine) and went to live in Germany.

He had been in Berlin for less than two years, writing and supporting himself as a Hebrew teacher and an editor in a Jewish publishing house, when the war broke out. Although much of *To This Day* is indeed autobiographical (Agnon did, during the war years, report regularly to his draft board; did live in fear of being called up and sent to the front; did travel often between Berlin and Leipzig; did change rented rooms frequently; and did fall ill and have to be hospitalized), much of it is not. In many ways, Agnon's wartime experience was far better than his narrator's. Unlike Shmuel Yosef in *To This Day*, he was not paralyzed creatively by the war or socially isolated; on the contrary, he kept his publishing job, persisted in writing Hebrew fiction that won recognition and was even translated into German, and made and maintained a wide range of social contacts that included friendships with Martin Buber and the department store magnate Salman Schocken, his future literary patron.

Nor did Agnon hurry, like his narrator, to return to Palestine when the war ended in 1918. It was not until 1924, in fact, after taking a German-Jewish wife and fathering two children, that he decided to re-immigrate to Palestine and settle in Jerusalem, where he reverted to the religious Orthodoxy of his youth—and this, too, only after a fire had razed his home in the resort town of Bad Hamburg and destroyed his large library and his manuscripts, among them a draft of a first full-length novel to which he was never to return.

What is interesting about this in regard to *To This Day* is not only that the narrator's yearning for Palestine is considerably greater than was Agnon's in those years; it is also that his growing abhorrence, as the war progresses, for Germany and all things German was clearly not Agnon's then either. From a Jewish point of view, indeed, Germany was not the enemy in World War I. However to blame German militarism may have been for the war's onset, the German army's behavior toward the Jews of the Eastern-European territories it conquered was exemplary, certainly when compared to the barbarism of the Russians. Nor was there significant public anti-Semitism in wartime Germany itself. Jewish soldiers fought, died, and were decorated alongside Christians in the German armed forces, and wartime censorship kept anti-Semitic opinions out of sight.

To what, then, can we attribute the narrator's attitude toward Germany? It makes more sense when we recall that *To This Day*, the last of Agnon's completed novels,* appeared in 1951—that is, that it was written, not after World War I, but after World War II, and that in it Agnon was projecting extreme anti-German feelings back onto an earlier age. Nor is this the only thing that the date of the novel's composition helps to explain. *To This Day*'s puzzling ending, too, becomes more understandable when we consider that Agnon wrote it following the Holocaust and the establishment of the state of Israel and its successful war of independence. However one thinks of these two colossal events in Jewish history, it is impossible not to regard them together.

In the eyes of many of Agnon's contemporaries, they were regarded through the prism of historical causality. Israel, in this per-

---

* Agnon's unfinished novel *Shira* was published posthumously in 1979. His other novels are *The Bridal Canopy* (1931), *A Simple Story* (1935), *A Guest for the Night* (1939), and *Just Yesterday* (1945).

spective, was a direct consequence of the Holocaust and of what led up to it. Political Zionism originated as a reaction to the European anti-Semitism that climaxed in the Nazi genocide, and the infrastructure in Palestine that made Israel's establishment possible was largely built in the 1920s and '30s by Jews fleeing Hitlerism and anti-Semitic persecution. Moreover, after World War II a Jewish state was perceived as necessary by the Gentile world because of the need to find a home for Holocaust refugees and to ensure that the Jewish people never again met such a fate. Without Christian guilt for what had happened, so the argument went, there would never have been international support for the creation of Israel.

Although one can challenge the historical accuracy of some of these assumptions, they were commonly viewed then, as they are today, to be true. And by some in Agnon's milieu in Jerusalem, which was that of what was and still is known in Israel as the "national religious camp," Israel's link to the Holocaust was considered to be even more profound. Conceived of theologically, it was viewed as part of a divine plan for redemption in which the Jewish people had to be purged in the Nazi inferno before commencing the messianic ascent of which the birth of Israel was a first harbinger. As stated by a leading proponent of this school of thought, Agnon's Jerusalem contemporary Rabbi Tsvi Yehuda Kook, the son of Palestine's first chief rabbi, the religious thinker Abraham Isaac Hacohen Kook:

> The Jewish people was torn from the depths of the Exile and brought to Israel. The blood shed by the six million [victims of the Holocaust] was a terrible incision in the body of the nation. The Jews underwent an operation that, though divine, was performed by the Nazi fiends, [for] God's people had so adhered to the uncleanliness of the lands of the Gentiles that it had to be forcibly cut away and removed from their midst by great violence... By means of this cruel surgery, our lives are now revealed to be those of a reborn nation in a reborn land with a reborn Torah and reborn holiness.... We must recognize the cosmologically divine nature of the historical facts.

Kook's theodicy was radical, even if its image of an emergency Caesarian delivery leaned on biblical precedent. ("Has God ever before sought," asks the book of Deuteronomy about the Exodus from Egypt, "to take a people from the midst of a people with trials and signs and wonders and war and a mighty hand and an outstretched arm and great terrors?") Many, probably most, "national religious" Jews would have shied away from such an extreme formulation, according to which the mother, the Jewish Diaspora, had to be killed for the child, the state of Israel, to be born. Yet they, too, would have agreed that this state was, if not a justification of the Holocaust in Kook's sense, a divine compensation for it, *reshit tsmihat ge'ulateynu*, "the first budding of our redemption," in the words of the "national religious" prayer book. Furthermore, this belief had its counterpart in Israel's secular political and intellectual establishments, whose supersessionist outlook held that if a doomed European Jewry had to perish for a Jewish state to emerge, the price, however dreadful, was worth paying. Israel was living through heady times. Despite the economic hardship of the post-independence years, the country was developing by leaps and bounds, absorbing large numbers of immigrants, making the wasteland bloom, throbbing with dynamism and confidence. The Holocaust was rarely a subject of public discussion. Though the crematoria had, as it were, just stopped smoking, their fallen ashes were already regarded as the historical matrix from which the Jewish future had sprung.

It is in this context that *To This Day* must be read. When it is, the full range of its symbolic equivalences becomes clearer. Although the events of the novel are not reducible to allegory, they also point to something other than themselves: World War I to World War II, the massacres of Jews in Galicia to the Holocaust, the narrator's return to Palestine and building of a home there to the Jewish people's creation of Israel, his concluding remarks to Holocaust-rationalizing Zionist theodicies and interpretations of history.

These remarks are indeed absurdly egocentric. They are Agnon's satirical protest against the belief that the state of Israel, however remarkable an achievement, is the end-all of Jewish history in the light of which all else can be rationalized. Like Voltaire's Dr. Pangloss, for whom everything from the torture chambers of the Inquisition to the devastation of the Lisbon earthquake turns out to have been for the best because he and Candide are now eating "preserved citrons and pistachio nuts" in their garden, there were those in the gardens of Agnon's Jerusalem who, unable to conceive of the Holocaust as a pure manifestation of evil serving no purpose in an arbitrary world, construed it as divinely or historically ordained. The ending of *To This Day*, put in the mouth of a narrator whose self-congratulatory preening is impervious to what was up to that point the greatest mass slaughter in the history of mankind, is a scathing critique of this outlook.

But it is also scathing toward Agnon himself, for just as Shmuel Yosef the narrator is a partial projection of Agnon the author, so a part of Agnon, yearning to believe in God's providential love for his chosen people, was tempted to embrace the narrator's point of view. He was restrained from this by the other part of him, Shmuel Yosef Bach the skeptic, who would have scoffed at such naive credulity. All of Agnon's large literary production, indeed, can be viewed, in one way or another, as an argument between the two Shmuel Yosefs. In it faith battles with unbelief, the ideal of religious wholeness with pitiless ironic laughter. We, Agnon's readers, are batted back and forth between them.

In everything he wrote, Agnon plays with us, and readers who resent being played with will not be among his principal admirers. Still, they too might concede that being asked to play with a master is no small compliment. Yes, Agnon often sets out to fool us. He deviously hides what is important and dangles before us what isn't. He entangles us in his net and smiles as we flounder there. But in the end, he trusts us to free ourselves and to profit from the exertion of doing so. If he didn't, he would have been foolish himself to write as he did. For this he deserves our trust in return, there being no riddle in his fiction to which he fails to provide, no matter how cleverly concealed, the clue to its solution. When we have finished following *To This Day*'s many loops, we find ourselves a surprisingly long way from where we started. It's enough to make one want to repeat the journey.

Chapter one

During the Great War, I lived in the west of Berlin, in a room with a balcony in a small boarding house on Fasanenstrasse. The room was small too, as was the balcony, but for someone like me whose needs were few it was a place to live. Not once during my stay there did I speak to the landlady or the other boarders. Every morning a chambermaid brought me a cup of coffee and two or three slices of bread, and once a week she brought the bill, which grew larger as the slices of bread grew smaller and the coffee lost its taste. I left the rent on the tray with a tip for her. She knew I didn't like small talk and came and went without a word.

Once, however, she forgot herself and stayed to chat a bit about the boarding house. Its landlady, Frau Trotzmüller, was a widow whose husband had been killed in a duel, leaving her with three daughters and a son, her youngest child, who had disappeared at the front. No one knew if he had been killed or taken prisoner. Despite all the family's efforts to trace him, nothing was known of his fate. Multitudes of soldiers were dead, captured, or missing in action; who could locate a single mother's son, a speck of dust swept away by the winds of war? Frau Trotzmüller and her daughters didn't impose their grief on their boarders, and their boarders didn't inquire about young Trotzmüller. Everyone had his own troubles; no one had time for anyone else's. It was only because I was a poor sleeper that I heard the grieving mother sobbing for her son at night.

There was another occasion, too, when the chambermaid told me about the boarding house. Its largest room, she said, was occupied by a wealthy young lady from the provinces who had come to attend finishing school. Across from her lived an official in the Tax Bureau, while next to him was an elderly couple who had fled the war zone. The remaining rooms belonged to lodgers who came regularly to Berlin on business. If I'm telling you things I never asked to be told about myself, it's only to explain that I couldn't switch to a better room because there were no vacancies.

The boarders were well behaved and quiet. Even the young lady from the provinces hardly made any noise when she had a birthday party and invited all her friends. I don't believe this had anything to do with our landlady's grief. It was the war itself that made everyone speak softly. While German artillery was being heard around the world, the Germans were talking in whispers.

When the war broke out, I stopped working. I even put aside my big book on the history of clothing. I couldn't write a thing as long as the fighting went on. All I wanted was to crumple the days into as small a ball as possible until it was over. In this way, a winter went by, and then a summer, and then another winter.

When spring came again, I could feel my room getting smaller. Half of it was perpetually dark and half was perpetually cold, and neither got any sunlight. There's a saying that not even the sun likes living in darkness, and I suppose that's what kept it from my room. And I, who had lived in Palestine and knew what a real sun was like, had a craving for light. Yet each time I stepped out on the balcony to warm up I had to retreat inside at once, since the trees were full of dust that the breeze blew everywhere and there were no street sweepers because of the war. Trees planted to make life better were only making it worse. Man, says the Bible, is a tree of the field. That must be why the trees join in when men go to war and spread misery.

So much for my room. As for myself, I should mention that I had no summer clothes or shoes. The more war refugees there were, the more appeals there were to donate clothing. I had given away all my summer things and couldn't buy new ones when the warm weather returned, because the tailors and shoemakers left in Berlin only made uniforms and army boots. Although this didn't matter as long as I stayed indoors, my clothes weighed on me as soon as I went out. And so I spent most of my time in my room, going from its cold half to its dark half, neither of which had any air or light because the trees outside blocked the sun and scattered dust. Even the rain was more dust than water.

God knows how long I might have gone on living in the cold, dust, and darkness of Berlin had not Dr. Levy's widow asked to consult with me about her husband's books, which she didn't know what to do with.

Not that travel was simple when staying in one place was so difficult. Nothing in the country was functioning normally; the smallest journey was an ordeal. The trains didn't run on time and were infrequent and crowded. And if you managed to find a seat, you still had to show your papers to the police. I won't bother to tell you what the police, a nasty lot in peacetime, were like in wartime.

And that wasn't all. Everything was rationed; there were vouchers for every bit of food, and those good for one place weren't good for another. Anyone traveling without a special ration book could die of hunger. There were excellent reasons for staying put.

And yet there was Dr. Levy's widow, all alone with a library that was too much for a woman like her and anxious to consult with me. And so, despite the hardship of travel, my fond memories of her husband made me decide to visit her. I thought of Dr. Levy's town, which I last had seen as his guest before the war. It was a quiet, peaceful place called Grimma, and the days spent in the two rooms of his library had been pleasant. How could I refuse a request to go there now?

I began to prepare for my trip. First, I went through my belongings to see what I needed and what I didn't and could throw out. Then I reviewed my manuscripts. I took my book on the history of clothing and read it all, discarding every page that wasn't crucial and even snipping off the margins to reduce its size. When I was done, I told the chambermaid I was leaving and went to the police station for a travel permit. Then I returned to my room to make sure I hadn't forgotten anything. I was waiting to set out for the station when the chambermaid knocked and asked if I had a few minutes to talk to the landlady. I glanced at my watch and went to see Frau Trotzmüller.

The only time I had ever spoken to Frau Trotzmüller was on the day I rented my room, when she and her daughters came to welcome me. She was a woman of about fifty, with a blond head streaked to the top with gray hairs. When she was young she must have been pretty, perhaps even beautiful, and something of that beauty had remained, though her eyes had a washed-out look. I supposed that came from crying at night for her son.

As I say, I had met her that day with her daughters. There were three of them, each odder-looking and stranger-sounding than the next. Lotte, the eldest, was a stout brunette with a complexion the color of burned fat. Although she was the tallest, this was hidden by her girth, all the more so because she hunched her head between her shoulders and peered up at you when she talked, interrupting her mother in a babyish lisp. Her sister Hildegard was thinner, with pitch-black hair, a narrow forehead, and prominent cheekbones, above which her eyes had to struggle to be seen; her voice had a hard edge to it, and it was she who ran the household and the boarding house. As for the youngest, Gert, she was slim like Hildegard, a freckled, coppery redhead with a nose the size of a barleycorn that sometimes vanished amid her freckles and sometimes jutted up saucily, and an unfinished slit of a mouth from which nothing ever emerged, since each time it opened to speak her sisters shushed her by saying: "Just look at her, hatched yesterday and already wanting to chirp!" I believe I've said enough about the three of them—and if it surprises you that I remember them at all, it shouldn't. In those days, I had so little contact with the world that I can recall every person I met. A mere name, face, or even smell can bring back an entire conversation.

Frau Trotzmüller was seated on a narrow divan when I entered her room, together with her daughters. Lotte was on her right and

Gert was on her left, and Hildegard was watering a potted cactus with her back to me.

Frau Trotzmüller held out her hand and asked me to have a seat. Then she ran the hand through her hair, as though checking for each gray and blond strand, while Gert glanced back and forth between us. Hildegard turned to her mother, her eyes widening above her cheekbones. "I hear you're leaving us," Frau Trotzmüller said. "I wanted to wish you a good trip. I couldn't decide whether to go to your room, so Hildegard suggested inviting you here. Thank you for coming."

"I, too, wanted to say goodbye and to thank you for your kindness," I replied. Frau Trotzmüller's face lit up and she asked if I had enjoyed my stay.

"If I weren't obliged to leave," I said, "I'd gladly stay here forever."

She let out a sigh and clasped her hands in sorrow.

I couldn't imagine what made her so sorry. Surely, it wasn't my moving out. There was no need to fear my room remaining empty. With every house in Berlin full of refugees, it would be snapped up in no time.

To break the silence, I pointed to the cactus that Hildegard was watering and said, "In this country, you grow a plant like that in a pot and treat it with love. Where I come from, it's only good for plowing up."

Lotte hunched her head between her shoulders, peered up at me, and lisped, "There must be all kinds of plants in your country that we don't know about." Hildegard gave Lotte a stern look and glanced encouragingly at her mother. Frau Trotzmüller, prompted by Hildegard's glance, regarded me with a sad smile and asked if I believed in dreams. Before I could guess what was on her mind she said, "I never believed in them myself. And now that you're leaving us, I believe in them even less."

Not only were her words strange in themselves, they were even stranger in view of the fact that she had barely exchanged a word with me until now. I glanced at her daughters, hoping for an explanation, and saw that they were waiting for one from me.

"I, too, have dreams," I said. "If they're good ones I know they won't come true, and if they're bad ones they don't scare me. The worst dream is no worse than real life. In any case, I never try to interpret them. I'm not Pharaoh or Nebuchadnezzar, and there are no Josephs or Daniels in our age, even if their descendants are said to live in Vienna. Not that I have anything against them, but their theories aren't for me."

Hildegard's eyes widened again and she said, "You must have heard that our little brother was sent to the front and hasn't been heard from." Frau Trotzmüller nodded and repeated, "He hasn't been heard from. He's disappeared."

"So I've heard, *meine Frau*, so I've heard," I answered. I couldn't think of what else to say. I glanced at the grandfather clock on the wall and then stared at the wall itself.

Lotte hunched her head and lisped, "Are you in a hurry to get to the station?"

I took out my pocket watch. "If my train leaves on schedule," I said, "I have time."

"Then perhaps you'll listen to mother's dream," said Hildegard. "Mother, tell him what you dreamed."

"Are your bags packed?" asked Frau Trotzmüller.

"Packed and ready to go," I said.

"Now that all the porters have been drafted," she said, "you won't find anyone to take them. And you'll never find a cab, either. Gert, go tell the doorman that your mother would like him to bring the gentleman's bags to the station and stay by his side until he comes for them."

Gert's little nose jutted up and the slit of her mouth opened as if to say, "Mother, I want to hear your dream, too." Hildegard looked at her sternly and scolded, "What are you sitting there for? Do as your mother says." Gert rose and went to get the doorman.

Frau Trotzmüller ran a hand through her hair and said, "I had the strangest dream. I've already told you that I don't believe in dreams, and now I have even less cause to. They say they're like soap bubbles and I agree, especially since you're leaving us. In my dream, my son came home. And not only did he come home, he came home because of you, *mein Herr*. Now that you're leaving us, I can see it's all one big soap bubble."

I sat trying to think of what to say to something like that. The clock chimed and I saw it was time to go. By now Gert had returned with the doorman. "You should be on your way, *mein Herr*," said Frau Trotzmüller. "Have a good trip."

I said goodbye to her and her daughters, gave my bags to the doorman, and followed him to the station.

Chapter two

I arrived at the station and fought my way onto the train. The car was packed with passengers: war provisioners, ersatz products dealers, military nurses, officers' mistresses, and amputees back from the front with their crutches, empty sleeves, rubber limbs, glass eyes, noses fashioned from buttocks by plastic surgeons, and terrified and terrifying faces that had lost their human features in the war. All were traveling with baggage—suitcases, duffle bags, bundles, boxes. You couldn't find your arms and legs in the crush.

The car smelled bad. There was no ventilation, all the window straps having been stolen. Everyone had to make his own air, which some did with cigarettes and others with cigars, pipes, and ersatz tobacco. The train jerked so hard that you couldn't tell if it was going forward or backward. The wheels rattled and shook; the pistons pounded up and down, drowning out the voices of the passengers. It took several hours to reach Leipzig.

I grabbed my bags and ran to catch the train for Grimma only to find that it had pulled out. The train from Berlin was late and the Grimma train hadn't wanted to wait. Not having the patience to wait in the station for the next train either, I checked my bags and looked for the exit to the city.

The din in the large station was deafening. Trains came and went, hissing and clanging. Porters and conductors ran between the tracks and locomotives, vanishing in clouds of steam and reappearing among the cars. It was like being in a city of steel, with steel houses that ran on steel wheels with a clatter of steel beneath a sky of smoke. The whole station was on the run; no one stopped to catch his breath. You couldn't make out a face amid all the faces.

An army transport was slowly unloading wounded soldiers for placement in local hospitals. The orderlies and nurses performed their jobs with aplomb; they had been through it before and knew just what to do. Only the wounded weren't yet accustomed to their pain. Nearby stood another train that was leaving for the front. The departing soldiers' families stood around them. Although you would have thought that by now they would have been used to it, they wept as though for the first time.

Suddenly I heard my name called. I turned around and saw an attractive, elegantly dressed woman holding out her hand with a bright smile. No one else had a smile like Brigitta Schimmermann's. Before I could say hello she said, "My husband and I are lunching at one-thirty. We'd love to have you join us. You will come, darling, won't you?"

"That," I said, "is a perfectly unnecessary question. In my wildest dreams I would never have dreamed of anything like this. Of course I'll come, my dear, of course I will. Without a doubt."

"If I weren't busy now," Brigitta said, "I'd ask you to spend the morning with me. But there's a fresh detachment of wounded and I have to see to their transfer to my nursing home. There are twelve cars full of them and I can barely handle one. When the historians sit down to write about this war, they'll have to invent a new language. The word 'man' will be replaced by 'invalid.' Yesterday I was brought a walking zombie who makes all the others look healthy, a perfect golem. But I'm in a hurry, darling, and I can't tell you everything at once. We'll talk over lunch."

"I only wish, Brigitta," I said, "that the hours until then would go by as quickly as I'd like them to. Give my best regards to Herr Schimmermann. I'll be there at one-twenty-five sharp."

Brigitta smiled her sweet smile. "Don't be late," she said. "I'll see you then."

I had to laugh. As if I might be late to a meeting with Brigitta Schimmermann! Just running into her was a joy, let alone being invited to lunch with her instead of having to look for a restaurant in this frantic wartime city in which you never knew what you were being served.

You must have heard of Brigitta Schimmermann, if only because of her decoration by the Kaiser for opening a nursing home and caring for the wounded like a true sister of mercy. I myself knew Brigitta from long before that, from the days when the world was at peace and she was an actress in a small theater company. Though her talents weren't great, she had a charm that made the critics treat her kindly. And Brigitta, while aware that her abilities were modest, knew there was something special about her and was content to be herself without resorting to the tricks of her trade. Watching her in the theater was like being in a living room with a lovely and gracious young ingénue. Since her father was a rich banker, she had no need for patrons and never fawned on anyone.

As a rule, pretty young actresses remain on stage until they find a husband. After several years, Brigitta caught the fancy of Gerhard Schimmermann, the son of Rudolf Schimmermann, a partner in a large munitions firm. She accepted Gerhard's proposal and they were wed.

Once Brigitta was married, she gave up her acting career. Yet her home was always open to artists and intellectuals and was known for its charity soirées. I remember how, on one such evening, she recited a tragic poem that brought tears to everyone's eyes. When the war broke out and the wounded and maimed were everywhere, she established a nursing home to look after them.

As I've said, I knew Brigitta from her stage days. At the time I was already at work on my universal history of clothing, and hearing

of me, she made me her costume adviser. Her dressmakers were aston-
ished to see her consulting someone like myself, who was far from a
smart dresser. They must have thought me a prince in disguise and
my armoires the secret source of her wardrobe.

Having no business in Leipzig, where I was stranded because
my train from Berlin had been delayed, I had time until my lunch
with Brigitta Schimmermann. To help pass it, I left the train station
and walked into town. After several blocks of shops and buildings
I came to the Brody Synagogue, which was founded by merchants
from across the Polish border who came every year to the Leipzig Fair.
Further on was another Polish synagogue and beyond that yet another
that had broken away from the first and named itself for General
von Hindenburg, perhaps in the hope of vanquishing its rivals as he
had vanquished the enemies' troops. The thought of troops made me
think of all the people I knew in Leipzig. Some were now at the front
and those who weren't lived in fear for those who were.

I came to Rosental Park. Young mothers walked hand-in-hand
with their children or wheeled them in carriages, making sure they
got plenty of fresh air so that they could grow up to be healthy young
men and go to war like their fathers.

Near the park was a neighborhood of fine homes half-hidden
by trees and gardens. In my Leipzig days I had been a regular visitor
in some of them. I was especially close to Dr. Mittel, a shrewd old
man and first-rate scholar whose *Bibliography of Oenology* had made
his reputation. He had even put me in a footnote in its revised second
edition because of a story I once published under the title "In Vino
Veritas." To this day I don't know whether he mistakenly thought I
had written a scholarly article about wine or was just making a friendly
gesture. According to my friend Mikhl Rabinovich, he was playing a
practical joke on his fellow bibliographers, knowing they would copy
the reference blindly as they always did from his books. Now, having
nothing better to do, I decided to drop in on him.

But before I tell you about our meeting, allow me to play the
storyteller and tell you about Mittel.

Isaac Mittel, better known as Dr. Mittel, came from a small,
heavily Hasidic town in Poland and was raised in a Hasidic fam-

ily. When he grew up, he abandoned religion and became a Communist. The Czar's secret police got wind of it and he was forced to flee to Germany, where he settled in Leipzig. There he started a new life, studied for his high school diploma, went on to university, and obtained a doctoral degree.

In his student days, Mittel earned a living by clerking in bookstores, dealing in old books, teaching Hebrew to Christian divinity professors, proofreading Hebrew texts for publishers, and serving as a guide for the Polish merchants who came to Leipzig for the fair. Through the latter he met some local Jewish businessmen, on whom his manly bearing, wit, and sterling qualities made a good impression. Hearing that he socialized with Christian professors—that is, with real Germans such as they, Germans citizens of the Mosaic faith, never rubbed shoulders with—they befriended him and invited him for coffee and dinner to their homes, where he became a frequent guest. In this fashion he met the daughter of a wealthy family and married her. Her large dowry made him financially independent, and he took to building a library and engaging in bibliographic research that became known for its thoroughness and reliability. Having to be reliable kept him honest and having to be thorough kept him on his toes.

Here I'll say a word about the profession of bibliography. There are bibliographers who systematically compile lists of books, authors, and dates and places of publication, and there are those who read for their pleasure, jot down what interests them, and eventually publish their notes. "I," Mittel liked to say, "have been both kinds. I used to catalogue books for bookstores and now I do it for myself." I hope I've given you some idea of this clever man, whose greatest ambition was to sit at home with his books.

Before paying him a call, it occurred to me to bring him a gift. All I could find in the store I entered was a bottle of seltzer. Well, then, I thought, I'll bring Mittel some seltzer. When there's a war going on and people are hungry, seltzer, too, is a gift.

I climbed the stairs, whose carpet was threadbare, rang a rusty bell, and waited. After a while the door opened a crack and Dr. Mittel appeared in an old jacket, regarding me with a mixture of curiosity and suspicion. All the books he had read had affected his sight and he failed to recognize me. Yet just as he was about to send me away, his curiosity got the better of his suspicion and he asked, "What can I do for you?" I reminded him who I was and said, "If you're busy, I'll be on my way."

Mittel seized my arm and steered me inside. "Did you say busy?" he asked with a laugh. "Busy, you say? Don't you know that our only business these days is doing nothing? Sit down, my friend, sit down. I suppose you've already ransacked every bookstore in Leipzig and left nothing even for the mice, and then remembered this old man at the last minute and decided to see if he was still alive. What's new in the world? Anything besides killing and being killed? First men go mad and start a war and then the war goes on by itself. My only son is fighting in it, too. In case you've never seen him, here's a photograph. Doesn't he look the hero in his uniform? A world conqueror! His dear mother has good reason to be proud of him. I never thought I would be the father of a soldier."

Mittel, who had a memory that never forgot a single title, had forgotten my visit on the day his son left for the army. I remembered the boy's mother scrutinizing every item that he packed in his kitbag, her eyes bright with joy at the sight of her boy going off to defend the Fatherland. That same day Mittel told me one of his stories about the author and publisher Heshl Shor, which I'll skip to avoid getting sidetracked. I'll only say that it was then, and on the next day, that I helped the rabbi of the Von Hindenburg Synagogue, Nachum Berish, prepare writs of divorce for the wives of Russian Jewish soldiers who were prisoners in Germany. They had been put to work in the coal mines and taken up with Christian women, making their marriages null and void.

"But let's forget about the world," Mittel went on, "and I'll tell you some real news. You know, Rabbi Boruch of Mezhibov was very wise when he said, 'The only justification for wars is that they make musicians write marches that my Hasidim turn into holy melodies that are sung at my table at the end of the Sabbath.' A week ago I received a letter from Hirsmann. What did it say? He had received a shipment of books that he thought might interest me and he wrote, 'If your legs happen to take you to the street my store is on, do drop in.' I read the letter and thought: as if Hirsmann doesn't know that legs don't go anywhere without being told! And so I dressed, slipped out of my slippers and into some shoes, and told my legs to take me to Hirsmann's store.

"On my way I encountered Herr König. He saw me and said, 'What good luck to run into you like this!' I said, 'Call it luck if you want, but what's so good about it?' König said, 'All my life I've worked on redesigning the Hebrew letters. Now I've finally located a foundry to cast the type—and here you are, in the nick of time for me to show it to you.' I asked, 'And who is going to publish the books you set in your type?' 'Publishers,' he said, 'I already have.' 'In that case, Herr König,' I said to him, 'you can see how unfairly I've been treated. I've been accused of being ungenerous toward the younger generation of bibliographers—but not only can they have their share of the books you print, they can have my share too, because I don't even want to look at them.' He said, 'But you should!' I said, 'I'm afraid my eye-glasses are too accustomed to the old letters to appreciate your new ones. Still, I'm happy you've succeeded.' 'You don't look happy,' he said. I said, 'Saying is the same as looking. That's why, when God gave the Torah on Mount Sinai, the Bible tells us, "All the people saw the voices." I'll tell you something else, too. Once someone brought Rabbi Shneur Zalman of Ladi a new book on Hasidism. He looked at it and said, "I see the letters, but where is the book?" In your case, Herr König, I haven't seen the letters, but I can imagine the books that will be printed with them.' After taking my leave of König, I kept my head down to keep from being recognized. Leipzig is a city of fairs and you never know who'll turn up with his merchandise. One man makes ersatz letters, another ersatz food, another ersatz arms and legs, and the Reich makes ersatz men and calls them soldiers. To tell you the truth, my friend, this is turning into an ersatz story. I'd better get back to Hirsmann.

"I came to Hirsmann's store. He had some books to show me that had arrived from conquered territory in Russia. I cleaned my glasses, reached into a pile, and pulled out some prayer books. Although they were of no importance to a bibliographer, they had been important enough to the Jews who had prayed from them. On the other hand, now that those Jews no longer had them, they had plenty of time to read war novels."

Mittel laughed a hoarse, jagged laugh. There was anger and anguish in it. Although I was sure he was about to vent his fury on modern intellectuals, as he was wont to do at such times, he restrained himself. His story, it seemed, mattered more to him than his anger.

He said, "I reached into the next pile. This time I came up with another prayer book, a Yiddish collection of women's devotions, and the Slavita edition of the *Zohar*—also no great cause for excitement. And what I found in them when I opened them, such as a pair of spectacles in the prayer book and some gray hairs in the *Zohar*, was nothing to write home about either, even if the devotions were half washed away by tears. I put them down and went on to another pile. It wasn't worth invading Poland for such stuff. One item was yet another little prayer book in which was stuck a piece of parchment with a handwritten plea to God to make the writer a better Torah scholar. What else was there? Ah, yes: a Jerusalem wall plaque, an illustrated Scroll of Esther, and some decorations for a Sukkah, the kind we made when we were children. By now I had had enough of this plunder, taken from poor Jews driven from their homes and robbed of all that was dear to them. Yet since a bibliographer can't keep his hands to himself, I kept rummaging through pile after pile. Finally, I fished from one of them a book of dirges for the Ninth of Av in an unknown edition. That is, it was an edition I had seen when I was young and had written about, and that Steinschneider mentioned in a footnote with an exclamation point as if to say, 'So says Mittel, and you can believe him if you care to.' You know me well, my friend. I've never wished anyone ill. Still, at that moment I couldn't help feeling sorry that Steinschneider was dead, because had he been alive, the one to feel sorry would have been him.

"But it was the next book I picked up that made me feel faint. I needn't tell you that there are towns all over Europe, some so small you won't even find them on the map, in which Jews were printing books when their Christian neighbors didn't know the alphabet. If someone were to bring me a Hebrew volume older than the Gutenberg Bible, it wouldn't surprise me in the least. After all, movable type was invented in China, and the Mongols possessed printed books long before anyone in Europe had heard of them; who is to say Jews didn't copy the technique? We know the Mongols introduced Europe to gunpowder, which the Jews left for the Germans—but books, my friend, books were something Jews had a use for."

He broke out laughing and said:

"I'm not only a bibliographer, I'm a mind reader. And if you'd like, I'll read your mind. You're thinking that this old man has taken leave of his senses. Well, I may really be too old to see my theory confirmed. But you, my friend, will live to see it. Meanwhile, let me show you something you've never seen before."

While taking out an old text he had found, held in place by slabs of wood like those used by the early bookbinders, he related an amusing anecdote about two bibliographers—one of whom, though a scholar, had made several embarrassing mistakes, while the other had made only one, which was to think he was a scholar. Mittel was still talking when I saw that it was time for my lunch with Brigitta Schimmermann.

I rose to go. "What's the hurry?" he asked.

"I have a luncheon appointment," I told him.

"With Frau Schimmermann," he said.

"You *are* a mind reader," I declared.

"As a matter of fact," Mittel said, "she telephoned before you came."

"But if you knew I was in Leipzig," I said, "how come you didn't recognize me?"

"It was precisely because I did know," Mittel said. "I waited so long for you to come that I lost my sixth sense and didn't realize it was you. Intuition is everything, my friend."

I said, "But I never told Frau Schimmermann that I planned to visit you. How could she have guessed?"

"You must have told her and forgotten," Mittel said.

"I couldn't have," I said, "because I didn't know I was going to visit you, either."

"Then you should be ashamed for not knowing," he said. "Frau Schimmermann knows you better than you know your own self. Who else were you going to visit? Even someone like me, who never goes anywhere, would visit someone like me if he existed."

"What exactly did Frau Schimmermann tell you?" I asked.

"She told me," Mittel said, "that she had forgotten to tell you that she and her husband would be at the Lion's Den."

"Well, then," I said, "I'll be off to the Lion's Den. Where is it?"

"You're asking me?" Mittel said. "How would a stay-at-home like me know something like that? Let's look in the phone book."

Mittel looked in the phone book and couldn't find it. Then he went through all the hotels, inns, restaurants, pubs, and beer cellars in the yellow pages and couldn't find it there either. He gave me a baffled look, said, "I know Leipzig like the back of my hand and never heard of any Lion's Den," and called information. No one there knew a thing about it. "Maybe," I said, "it wasn't the Lion's Den. Maybe it was the Leopard's Perch, or the Antelope's Horns, or the Eagle's Wings, or some other place mentioned in the Bible."

Mittel made a wry face. "You're making fun of me. Frau Schimmermann will think I'm just a dumb Polack who can't be trusted with anything."

My stomach was beginning to growl. To calm it, I took a glass and poured myself some of the seltzer I had brought. Mittel said:

"Just look what we've come to! A Jew has a visitor and doesn't offer him food or drink. Soon my dear wife will come home and make us coffee. She's so busy feeding the world in that soup kitchen she volunteers in that she forgets she has a husband to feed, too. By now I'm used to fasting, but if I live to be a hundred I'll never get used to having a hungry guest in my home. The only reason I decided to keep a kosher kitchen was so that I could offer hospitality to every Jew. Even if it was time for prayer, we Kotzk Hasidim never asked a guest, 'Have you prayed?' before asking, 'Have you eaten?' I've spoiled your lunch, my friend. Wait until my wife comes home and she'll make you a meal in place of Frau Schimmermann's."

"I'd better go," I said.

"Where?"

"I'm on my way to Grimma."

Mittel looked disappointed and fell silent. Then he sighed and said: "I suppose you're going to see Levi's widow. If I weren't an infirm old man who hates travel and the company of women, I'd go with you. What will become of Levi's library? Who will use it now? The dealers will sell it off piecemeal. What a man that was! He had eyes that didn't need glasses until the day he died. They say you could see nothing wrong with him even as he lay dying and writing his will. When is the next train for Grimma? You still have two hours, don't you? You may as well spend them with me. I'll put on something presentable and walk you to the station, although to tell you the truth, all the soldiers and cripples in the streets make me want to stay home. Sit down, my friend. Sit and I'll tell you a story.

"Perhaps you've heard of Shlomo Rubin. I knew the man and can tell you that his books were nothing compared to him. I heard many stories from him, one of which I'll pass on to you.

"There was once a tireless shoemaker who stayed up all night making shoes—cutting the leather and shaping the soles and stitching each shoe. One night an imp appeared and stuck out its tongue at him. The shoemaker took his knife and cut off the imp's tongue. The imp stuck out another tongue. The shoemaker cut that one off, too. To make a long story short, the imp kept it up and the shoemaker kept it up, and when morning came the shoemaker saw that every piece of leather in his shop had been slashed to pieces.

"Do you follow me? The Germans are tireless. They keep lashing out at their enemies and in the end they harm only themselves. This war won't end so quickly. The Germans are a stubborn people. Once they start something, they see it through. They began this war and they won't stop it until either they or their enemies are beaten. As far as I'm concerned, it doesn't matter who beats whom. Both sides are war-crazed and victory-mad. But if you ask me, the winners will be Germany's enemies, because they have numbers on their side.

"If I wrote fiction, I'd write a story set in the future. I'll tell you how it would end. Germany has been vanquished and divided up by the victors. Nothing is left of it but a tiny principality, and all that remains of the Germans is a small, destitute people. They're so poor they can only think of where their next meal will come from. Their universities and libraries are converted into tenements and all their books and works of art are burned for heating and cooking. In the end, not a page survives from all of German literature and philosophy. You say one war couldn't do that to a great nation? But one war leads to another. After a second war and a third war, the Germans have been beaten to their knees. There's no more talk of victory or fighting on. All anyone wants is a bit of food to eat, some clothes to wear, and a roof over his head.

"Time goes by. Little by little, the life of the mind resumes—and with it the memory of how once there were great poets and philosophers whose work has vanished because it was used to heat ovens. From afar comes a rumor that in a land called America live Jews who came there from Germany. And since Jews are traditionalists who preserve the languages of the countries they have lived in, they still know German and read German books. Messengers are sent to America to bring these books back to Germany, just as Hebrew books are now being brought from the conquered territories. And don't ask me, why go all the way to America when German is also spoken in Switzerland and in Austria and in other places, because this isn't a page of the Talmud whose logic has to be impeccable. If you weren't in such a hurry, I'd flesh it all out for you. If I'm still alive when you pass through Leipzig again on your way back from Grimma, I'll do it then. And though you may think this is pure fiction like any tale about the future, you have my word that it's perfectly true."

Chapter three

I returned to the station, picked up my bags, and squeezed into the Grimma train. As bad as the trip was from Berlin to Leipzig, the trip from Leipzig to Grimma was worse. Worst of all was pulling into the station. Since it was wartime and every able-bodied man was in the army, the trains were run by women. Discovering they were subject to female rule, they declared their independence. Instead of stopping in the station, this one came to a halt forty or fifty meters short of it, and the more the women tried getting it to move, cursing and swearing furiously, the more it stood there belching black smoke at them. The smoke brought tears to their eyes but no pity to its heart, which was made of steel.

We were still far from the station with no porters or anyone else to help. I took my bags, dragged myself with them to the stationhouse, and went to check my big suitcase. The baggage room was shut. I left my bags by the door and went to find the person in charge. Along came an official, scolded me for leaving my bags illegally, and made me pay a fine. I moved them to another place and went to look for the baggage checker again. A man standing there said, "How can you leave your bags unguarded?" When I asked if he would mind guarding them, he shrugged and walked off. After a while, the baggage checker returned. I gave him my big suitcase, took the smaller one, went into town, and found a hotel.

The hotel owner glared at me. Either I, my suitcase, or the two of us failed to please him.

"Do you have a room?" I asked him.

"Do you have a passport?" he asked me.

I gave him my passport. Seeing that I was a foreigner he said, "I can't let you have a room without a police permit."

"Where is the police station?" I asked.

"Ask anyone in the street," he said.

There was no one in the street to ask, since whoever wasn't at the front was at home or in some factory producing war goods. The day was ending; a thick gloom rose from the earth to meet the darkness dropping from the roofs of the munitions plants. I strained to see in the fading light and spotted a man standing by a streetlamp. "Where are the police?" I asked him. At once he took to his heels. It seemed I had raised a delicate subject.

In the end, I found the police station on my own. The policemen were busy boozing and berated me for barging in on them. Drunk though he was, one of them, when handed my passport, kept his wits sufficiently about him to swear a blue streak at Germany's enemies, who were everywhere. "But I'm an Austrian," I said. "I'm your ally. I only need a permit for my hotel." He took out a permit, fanned his schnapps-flushed face with it, reached for a pen, and wrote: "The bearer may reside in Grimma for three days."

I returned to the hotel and showed the owner my permit. He led me to a room with a bed. It was an ordinary room with an ordinary bed, except that it had a stale smell and the bed was broken. Still, after a hard day's traveling, any bed will do to rest one's bones on.

I lit a cigarette to drive away the smell and calm my stomach, which was complaining again. When I finished the cigarette, I sipped some water and went to bed without supper. It was pointless to ask for any, because I would only have been told that it was late and there was nothing to eat.

I've already told you I have trouble sleeping. Being in an ornery German's hotel didn't help. I tried adjusting myself to the broken bed by lying in a broken line and thinking of other things, such as my room in Berlin. Then, since that was no paradise either, I reviewed the day's events. I pictured Brigitta Schimmerman in the crowded train station, holding out her hand with a smile and inviting me to lunch. In the end, not only did I go without lunch, I went without supper, too. What had brought me to this place? A letter from Dr. Levi's widow, the two rooms of his library, and the vague hope of finding a room in the country for the summer.

And as if the bed beneath me and the hunger inside me weren't enough, I now began to worry about the future ahead of me. To take my mind off it, I tried thinking of the different combinations that could be made from the letters of Hebrew roots. Since my main worry was getting through the night, I chose the letters *bet-kuf-resh*, which spelled *boker*, morning. Switch them around and they spelled *rakav*, rot. Switch them again and they spelled *krav*, battle. Switch them once more and they spelled *kever*, grave.

I looked for roots with more pleasant associations. *Ayin-nun-gimmel* gave me *oneg*, enjoyment, which could be turned into *nega*, infection. *Shin-peh-ayin* was *shefa*, abundance, which yielded *pesha*, crime. *Shin-peh-resh* produced *shefer*, loveliness, which became *refesh*, filth. And on the other hand, there was *emet* and *tsedek* and *hesed*, whose truth, justice, and lovingkindness never changed because you couldn't make anything else from them. Little by little my eyes grew heavy until, thinking of *halom*, dream, I fell asleep and dreamed of war, *milhama*.

In the morning, I asked for a cup of coffee. What I was given was not only not coffee, it wasn't a substitute for a substitute for coffee. And since Frau Trotzmüller's dream had made me forget to ask her for a ration book, I couldn't even buy a loaf of bread. All I could find to eat was some wormy fruit. I picked out the worms, ate a bit of the fruit, and went to see Dr. Levi's widow.

Her home, when I reached it, was locked. The house stood on a low knoll, set apart from the houses around it, in the middle of a garden that now looked like a briar patch. For a long while I stood there wondering how a woman whose husband had left her the finest garden I ever had seen could let it go to seed. I remembered strolling through it with Dr. Levi, picking fruit and marveling at his knowledge while the birds, loathe to interrupt his displays of erudition, soared in silence overhead. Now it was desolate, its flowers gone, its trees cut down, crows cawing from their stumps. Where was Frau Levi? Although I had always thought that wise men chose wise women, this woman had laid waste her husband's inheritance.

You know I'm not a man who thinks ill of the other sex, but seeing such neglect I couldn't help it. A dog came along and barked at me. I left it to its own devices and went to look for Dr. Levi's widow.

No one could tell me where she was. Some of the passersby I stopped answered questions I hadn't asked them and others had never heard of Dr. Levi. I saw I was getting nowhere and threw up my arms in despair. The heavens took note and clouded over, raining down on me without mercy. Looking for shelter, I spied a rickety shack buffeted by the wind. Some local residents had taken refuge inside it.

"Would anyone happen to know why Dr. Levi's house is shut down?" I asked them.

"There are all kinds of vagabonds around," one man said. "People lock their houses to be safe."

I drew myself up to my full height to show I wasn't a vagabond and explained that Dr. Levi's widow had asked to see me on urgent business.

A man was cleaning his pipe. "I've heard of that doctor," he said. "What kind of medicine did he practice?"

"I wouldn't go to him whatever kind it was," declared a shiftless-looking fellow who had just ducked in from the rain himself. "If you need a doctor, we've got a young one in town who's an ace. Everyone knows him. His mother is that blankety blank _____."

He used two words before her name that I'm too polite to repeat.

As I was standing there; the shack began to leak. To make matters worse, although the rain was clean, the water leaking from the roof was filthy. I went to look for another shelter and found one that was occupied, too. "Do you have any idea where I might find Dr. Levi's widow?" I asked the man inside. "No," he said. "But there's a Jewish grocer around here who might." When the rain let up, he pointed the way to the grocer's.

I inquired at the grocer's. In reply, he broke into a lament for the late Dr. Levi. And not only was Dr. Levi dead and gone, his wife was on her way to joining him. Some of the doctors said she had a growth in her intestine and some said she had something else. God created thousands of illnesses, and the doctors learned the names of them all and left it to God to cure them. Levi's widow was in the hospital, being tortured with all kinds of drugs. They were so expensive that she would never get out of debt even if she got out of the hospital. True, her husband had left her two rooms full of books, but meanwhile the mice would eat them. And even if they didn't, there wasn't a soul left who could read them.

I was getting hungry again. "I've forgotten my ration book," I said, "and no one will sell me any food."

The grocer made a wry face at the thought of a fool big enough to forget his ration book. But he said in a friendly tone:

"If you'll excuse my simple home, you can have lunch with us. Meanwhile, take a roll from the basket."

I helped myself to a roll and rose to go to the hospital in order to see Frau Levi. The grocer sought to dissuade me. "She's too ill for visitors," he said. Yet seeing that I was determined, he gave me directions for getting there.

Dr. Levi's widow lay in bed and didn't recognize me. Perhaps the war and its rationing had affected my looks and perhaps her illness had affected her mind. I reminded her of the letter she had written me and of my having been a guest in her home. Just as she seemed on the verge of remembering, a nurse stepped into the room and made me leave.

I walked back to the grocery store, told the grocer what had happened, and added that I was thinking of spending the summer in Grimma.

"Even if you found a room here," he said, "you'd never find room and board. There's no food available. The town has barely enough for itself and no one wants to share it with a stranger, especially if that stranger is a Jew."

"Once," I said, "Jews were disliked for no reason. Now there finally is one."

"I wouldn't say that," said the grocer. "Times are hard."

It's easier, I thought, for a country to level the world than for it to spare a slice of bread for a stranger. But I didn't say so. German Jews were great patriots and the grocer would have skinned me alive. "What's it like to be a Jew here?" I asked.

The grocer laughed. "What's it like to be a Jew? If the Christians didn't remind us, we'd forget that that's what we were."

"You too, *mein Herr*?" I asked.

"When it comes to that," the grocer said, "I'm a Jew like any other."

After shutting his store for the midday break, he brought me home with him and explained to his wife that I was a traveler who had forgotten his ration book and couldn't eat at his hotel. She greeted me warmly and said, "If you don't expect anything fancy, I promise you won't go hungry."

In no time the table was set and we sat down to eat. "If you had come before the war," the grocer's wife said, "I would have cooked you a real meal with all the trimmings. Now we have to make do with what we find in the market." She turned to her husband and said, "Tell him the story of Enshel."

"What's there to tell?" the grocer said, although he seemed eager enough to tell it. "I'm sure he's heard it already."

"Actually, I haven't," I said, although actually I had.

"I don't believe you," said the grocer, "but I'll tell you anyway. There was once a town in Germany whose Jews were so well-off that they had no one to give charity to. One day a poor Jewish traveler named Enshel passed through town. It was a chance to give alms and they did so generously. When Enshel was about to depart, the Jews realized they would miss him, and so they got together and founded an organization named the Enshel Society and made him agree to return every year. Each of them kept an alms box called the Enshel Box in his home, and once a year Enshel came to collect the proceeds."

After telling the story of Enshel, the grocer related to his wife that I was in Grimma to see Dr. Levi's widow. This led him to the subject of Dr. Levi—who, though a fine man, had had a temper that made him scold people for things that only he would have minded. You could blame his books for that, because he was a good person at heart and ready to do anything for others. It was the books, which filled two large rooms, that had made him so critical. The good Lord knew why he needed two rooms of them when even one room held more books than anyone had use for. Most likely he had started with a single book, and had then bought another, and hadn't been able to stop. Now all his books belonged to his widow, who was no longer in her right mind. There was no one to read them or go through their pages except for the mice. When the mice were done with them, there would be nothing left.

Quite evidently the grocer thought that books and mice were a good match. I don't recall how the conversation got around to Palestine. Perhaps I mentioned coming from there, since in those days I did so at every opportunity. Talking about it made my life away from it easier to bear, just as the thought of the journey's end, when all his troubles will be over, comforts the homesick traveler.

The grocer rose from the table, returned with a thin Hebrew book, and handed it to me. "I can't read this and I'm not a Zionist," he said. "Still, I keep it because it comes from Palestine and is printed in the letters of the prayer book."

I took one look at it and pushed it away. The grocer noticed and was puzzled that a Jew from Palestine should treat a Hebrew book like that. When I told him it was an anti-Zionist Hebrew book, he looked more puzzled than ever.

After our meal, my host offered me a cigar and we put Dr. Levi and Palestine aside and talked about the usual things that one talked about in those days. When my cigar had burned down to my fingers I said, "It's time I got back to my hotel." The grocer accompanied me. As we walked, he invited me to eat in his house for the rest of my stay in Grimma.

"Not having a ration book, I don't have much choice," I said. "If you didn't invite me, I'd have to invite myself."

He laughed and remarked, "They say nothing is as simple as it seems. Perhaps you forgot your ration book so that I could invite you."

The hotel wasn't far. The grocer entered it with me, gave the owner a friendly slap on the back that resounded throughout the lobby, and announced: "I want you to treat this man as if he were me. If I weren't concerned about your making a living, I'd put him up in my own home. Don't be a swine, old man. Feed him well and give him a decent bed."

The owner nodded obediently. You could see it was less because the grocer inspired deference than because he was in the habit of deferring.

I slept well that night. By now my bed and I were old friends. In the morning, when I went down to the dining room, I was given a proper breakfast. That changed everything. Once again I was tempted to spend the summer in Grimma, whether in a hotel or a rented room. Food, I now saw, was no problem. With a bit of connections and money, you could always find something to eat—and besides, food wasn't the point. It was peace and quiet I was looking for.

I left the hotel in a good mood, my body rested and satisfied and my mind made up. A man passed me in the street and growled, "*Russ!*" I don't have to tell you that I come from Austrian Galicia and am not a Russian, and that although *Russ* is not a dirty word in my vocabulary, that lout hadn't meant it as a compliment. Then and there I decided not to spend the summer in Grimma after all. I'd be better off in a big city like Berlin that was used to Jews.

I returned to the hospital to look in on Frau Levi. She was feeling better and was glad to see me. A day or two ago, she told me, a stranger had come to see her with some outrageous story about a letter asking to consult him about her husband's books. Never having written it, she knew at once he was a master swindler. The odd thing was that she had meant to write it and hadn't gotten around to doing it before falling ill. Not that she was as ill as all that. In fact, she would talk to the doctors today about curing her more quickly, since what else were doctors for? On second thought, though, it now occurred to her that she might have written a letter after all, although more probably to someone like me than to the man who had visited her yesterday. Since I was already in Grimma, why didn't I stay a few more days? She would soon be released from the hospital and we would see to her husband's books.

A tall, young doctor entered the room, a pleasant-looking man with a blond beard and kind face. Perhaps it was his mother who had been called an unmentionable name in the shack. He glanced at Frau Levi and gave me a commiserating look, as if I were a friend in distress. Either my winter clothes made him feel sorry for me, or he saw I felt sorry for Frau Levi, or he thought I pitied him for having such a mother. One way or another, he was trying to be sympathetic. Not wanting his sympathy, I left.

I returned to the grocer's and told him about seeing Frau Levi. Everybody knew, he said, that she hadn't a chance of recovering. From her illness he returned to the subject of her husband's books, which had no financial value, and from the books to Dr. Levi's dispute with those two eminences of German Jewry, the Reverend Rabbi Gesetztreu and the financier Hochmute, who had taken Levi to task for parading his Jewishness and being an outspoken Zionist. After a while the grocer shut his store and took me home with him for lunch.

This time, offered a cigar after the meal, I presented him with a box of cigars that I had bought for him. He glanced at it and said:

"I've given up smoking."

I said, "I envy you."

"Don't," he said. "You should envy me when I start again. That will be a red-letter day."

"What will be the occasion?" I asked.

He opened his jacket, showed me three cigars tucked into its breast pocket, and said:

"Do you see these cigars? I used to be a heavy smoker. There was a time when I smoked twelve, thirteen, fourteen cigars a day. When my three sons went off to war, two of them draftees and one a volunteer, I put these cigars in my pocket and said, the next time I smoke will be when my sons come home."

I wished them a safe and speedy return and him the resumption of his old habits.

"Amen," he said, while his wife wiped a tear from her eye.

In bed that night I definitely concluded that Grimma was not for me. In the morning I ate my breakfast, had something to drink, paid my bill, and went to the police station. A policeman stamped my permit and I continued to the train station, picked up my suitcase, and caught a train back toward Berlin.

Chapter four

There was no direct train to Berlin and I had to change again in Leipzig. Instead of waiting in the station, I checked my luggage and walked into town.

It was a spring day. The usual stench of the city, which gave Leipzigers sneezing fits most of the year, had yielded to balmier air. You could even make out the dull blue of the sky, which was the color of the fox furs sold at the Leipzig Fair. I strolled past the fancy shops, looking in their display windows at the hides and pelts of beasts come to town from the woods and fields. From there I walked to Rosental Park. I passed Mittel's house, decided not to disturb him, and sat down on a park bench. Across from me a woman was knitting and reading. A small boy, dressed as a soldier with a wooden sword, played in the dirt at her feet. Now and then, she glanced up from the book on her knees and returned to it. The park slowly filled with women and children. After a while I rose to make room for them and walked off. "You're a bad man!" the boy called after me.

What had I done? I had accidentally stepped on a chalk circle he had drawn on the pavement. "Believe me, little boy," I said, "I'm not bad at all and I can draw you an even bigger circle." But he had already forgotten both me and the circle. "Look, mama, look!" he cried, clapping his hands in glee. I followed his glance and saw a poodle in a vest standing in front of a new building. The building's entrance was flanked by stone lions and bore a sign that said "The Lion's Den."

I entered The Lion's Den. It would be too perfect, I thought, if Brigitta Schimmermann were suddenly to appear—but of course she never would, since no one turned up just when you wanted them to. On the other hand, since I was so certain that she wouldn't, perhaps she would.

A waitress came and asked, "What can I bring you, *mein Herr?*"

I ordered coffee and asked whether she knew Frau Schimmermann.

"Why, of course," she said. "I do all her ironing."

And had she come for lunch today?

"No," the waitress said, "not today. She was last here three days ago."

"And not only was she here three days ago," I told her, "she was here with Herr Schimmermann, and she asked for a table for three, and the third person didn't show up. You're looking at him now."

The waitress stared at me with working-class incredulity. Chagrined that I didn't look the type to lunch with Frau Schimmermann, I left a big tip to impress her. How impressed she was, I can't say, but it did make her think well enough of me to tell me where Frau Schimmermann might be found.

"On days when she isn't in Leipzig," she said, "she's at her nursing home for soldiers in the country."

I returned to the station, picked up my bags, and took a train to Lunenfeld, where Brigitta Schimmermann had her nursing home. The train ride took half an hour. Another half-hour's walk brought me to the nursing home. Before the guard at the gate could say, "Come back another time," Brigitta spied me. "You're a naughty man," she said, holding out a finely shaped hand. "You made us wait and never thought we might be hungry. What wonders did you find in Leipzig to make you stand us up?"

"You don't know the half of my naughtiness," I said. "This is my second scolding in one day. First I was called bad by a little boy for stepping on his chalk circle and now it's by you. But I'm not to blame if The Lion's Den isn't listed in the phone book."

"This," Brigitta said, "is not the time for your court-martial. You'll stand trial over dinner. First, let me show you around. And before that we'll have something to drink."

She brought me to her office, ordered coffee, and said: "Tell me about your day in Leipzig. Whom did you see there?"

"I paid a call on Dr. Mittel," I told her. "How on earth did you think of phoning him? And what would you have done if I hadn't been there?"

Brigitta laughed and said, "I wouldn't have done anything different, because you didn't turn up anyway. As for Mittel, I had phoned to speak to his wife. When he began to grumble about being a victim of her volunteer work, I changed the subject to you."

The girl who had brought us coffee now returned with a visiting card. The head nurse, she said, had told her to give it to Frau Schimmermann. Brigitta glanced at it and said, "I have important guests and have to show them the nursing home. If I know you, you won't want to take the tour with them. What will I do with you in the meantime?"

"Don't worry about me," I said. "I have a cousin here in Lunenfeld. I'll pay her a visit."

"Just be back in time for dinner," Brigitta said.

"If God doesn't play another trick on me like the one he played in Leipzig, I certainly will be," I told her.

"In that case," said Brigitta, "you had better stay here. You can see your cousin tomorrow."

"Brigitta," I said, "have you no faith in God?"

"Faith in God," she said, "I have. Faith in you is something else. Here, why don't you take a look at this new volume of Van Gogh reproductions. It will keep you busy until dinner time."

"All right," I said. "I'll look at the reproductions before dinner and see my cousin after it."

"You must have a low opinion of yourself," Brigitta said, "if you think you have so little to say that dinner will end that quickly."

It felt like old times to be with Brigitta Schimmermann, even though the room we were in was not like her old place in Berlin. It was furnished in the wartime style, with faded fixtures and a photograph of the Kaiser on the wall. This was flanked by smaller photographs of Generals von Hindenburg and Mackensen, while a war map full of pins hung on another wall. On the desk was a portrait of Brigitta's small daughter, a vase of wildflowers, and several snapshots, one of them of the two Schimmermanns, Brigitta's husband Gerhard and his father. Next to it were some books. A recent German translation of Tolstoy's legends was opened to a page held in place by a plaster paperweight in the shape of a cannon.

The telephone rang and Brigitta went to welcome her guests. I remained in her office, looking at the reproductions. After a while I thought of my cousin, who had been living by herself since her husband and son were drafted. I put Van Gogh down and set out for her house.

On my way, I passed a young man in a field. Although he wasn't wounded, he had a wounded look and he regarded me in wonderment when I said hello. Not knowing that one didn't say hello to prisoners of war, I stopped to chat with him as if he were an ordinary person. This made him feel like one and he began to talk about himself. His father was dead and he was his mother's youngest child. When war broke out, he was drafted and sent to the front. After his battalion surrendered, he was shipped to Germany and indentured to a woman from Lunenfeld whose husband was at the front, too. The chores she made him do were like those he did for his mother, from whom he hadn't heard a word. He didn't know if she was alive or what was happening in the world, because no one spoke to him except to shout and give orders.

I stood there thinking of Frau Trotzmüller. If the young man hadn't been a Russian, I might have mistaken him for her missing son. Sensing my sympathy, he asked for a cigarette. I gave him all the cigarettes I had and wished I had more.

It was getting late and I returned to the nursing home. At dinner I told Brigitta about the Russian prisoner. She frowned and said, "You shouldn't have spoken to him. Someone might have seen you and told tales."

"But don't Germans realize," I said, "that tomorrow it could be their son who is a prisoner in Russia? How would they like it if he were treated as a pariah?"

Brigitta's frown darkened. "I'll have to ask you not to speak that way," she said. "War is war."

War here, war there, war everywhere. Because of the war you weren't allowed to pity or talk to a poor boy taken from his mother. Because of the war there were no longer human beings, just soldiers and officers and casualties and prisoners and enemies. That evening a wall rose between Brigitta Schimmermann and myself. Although we pretended not to notice it, a wall is a wall. Our conversation faltered for the first time in memory, and we parted in time for me to go to my cousin's.

It's hard to describe the joy of a woman who, the only Jew in her village, from which her husband and son have been taken, has a surprise visit from a cousin—and not just any cousin, but one she hasn't run into for years and thought she never would see again. When the people you see every day are snatched from you, how can you expect to meet a distant relative whom you haven't come across in ages? She was so excited that, despite having a thousand things to ask and to tell me, she couldn't think of a single one of them or do anything but feast loving eyes on me. Suddenly, she exclaimed with a worried look, "But you must be hungry! I'll wager you haven't had your supper. Let me throw something together for you."

"I'm not hungry at all," I said. "I just dined with Frau Schimmermann."

My cousin stared at me incredulously. In times like these, when all anyone could think of was his stomach, how could I not be hungry? Even if I had eaten, I couldn't possibly have eaten enough. She rose to go to the kitchen, stopped halfway there, came back to ask me something she had just thought of, forgot what it was, returned to the kitchen, and remembered she had run out of cooking gas. She had no kerosene either, only wood, and cooking with wood was so slow that a Jew's worst enemies should only have to wait so long for their food. To think that a long-lost cousin was her guest and she couldn't offer him a hot meal!

"I'm quite full," I said. "You could set the greatest delicacies before me and I wouldn't have room for them."

The more I protested, the more upset she grew. The minutes went by and I had to go. She wouldn't let me leave without making me swear to come back. "If this time I came to see you without an oath," I assured her, "you can be sure I'll come back now that I've taken one."

And now let me tell you about my cousin.

She came from a well-to-do family. Her father, though a religiously observant, well-educated Jew, had progressive tendencies that set him apart from the rest of his family, who never swerved from the trodden path of tradition. Having no sons, he took the unusual step of hiring a private tutor for his daughter and even of teaching her Hebrew. When she reached marriageable age, he found her a husband to her liking, the son of a country estate manager who was a Hebraist and a Zionist. Although she went to live with him in the Polish countryside, their dream was to buy land in Palestine and farm it. For some reason, however, they moved to Germany instead. After trying his hand at several businesses that failed, my cousin's husband purchased a chicken processing plant in Lunenfeld. Along came the war and he was drafted. Before leaving for the army, he moved his wife and son to a house in the country to economize. Time passed and the boy was called up too, leaving my cousin by herself. That was her story—to which I should add that she was fifteen years older than me. I only mention this because, should you find her naïve, bear in mind that hers was a generation in which naiveté was considered nothing to be ashamed of.

The next morning I went to see her again. Even though I had promised to return, her amazement had no bounds. It took her a while to calm down and to ply me with all the questions she had for me, most of which were about myself.

"Tell me what you want to know," I said. "I'll answer as best I can."

"There are so many things," my cousin said, "that I don't know where to begin."

I said, "Then begin anywhere."

"That's easy for you to say," she said. "I'll try. I've heard you write books. I remember you once wrote poems. There's nothing in the world I like better than a poem, especially when it rhymes. Prose just isn't the same."

"That's true if a poem is poetic," I said.

"How can a poem not be poetic?" she asked. "If you bought a prayer book that had no prayers, would you call it a prayer book? You'll have to explain yourself."

"It's hard to explain and even harder to understand," I said. "I'm talking about subtle intellectual matters."

"Do you think," she asked, "that living in the country has so addled my brains that I can't understand intellectual matters?"

"I didn't say that," I said. "It all depends on what you mean by intellectual."

Although I pretended to be testing her, I wasn't sure what I meant by it myself.

My cousin rubbed her eyelids with her thumbs and thought. After a while she said, "All right, I'll tell you."

"Please do," I said.

"An intellectual," she said, "is someone who can recite Psalms without tears."

I couldn't have put it any better myself.

That set her to talking. "You're dressed modern now," she said. "But I can remember you in Jewish clothes, with your curly earlocks bouncing up and down. I always felt sorry for your cheeks, because they couldn't get your earlocks to lie flat. How smooth they were! Wasn't it Jacob who said, 'My brother Esau is a hairy man and I am a smooth man'? I never put much stock in the Hasidim who curl their earlocks and think it makes them better than other Jews, but to tell you the truth, I'd rather live with them than with Germans. It's an odd thing. When I was in Galicia I wanted to live in Germany, and now that I'm in Germany I wish I were back in Galicia. Do you think that's because the grass is always greener somewhere else? Don't take it as a criticism of Zionism if I say that maybe that has something to do with it. You know I'd give my right arm to live in Palestine. Still, I sometimes can't help wondering whether that isn't all Zionism amounts to. I wish you'd say to me, 'Malka, you're wrong.' My husband and I have agreed that if God sees us safely through this war, we'll settle in Palestine. But you were already living there, so what made you leave? I hope it wasn't what I just said about no one being happy where he is. You can be honest with me. But I see you'd rather not talk about it. Fine, then. Let's talk about other things."

Although she would have liked nothing better than to go on discussing these doubts of hers, she reluctantly changed the subject. "What do you hear from your brother?" she asked. "I've heard he's in the army, too. If this war doesn't end soon, there won't be a Jew left out of uniform. And there are Jewish soldiers on the Russian side too, fighting their own flesh and blood. Good, decent Jews, people you would be glad to have for your neighbors, suddenly start a war with you! Do you understand it? I don't. For whom are they fighting? For a Czar who slaughtered them in his pogroms. And against whom? Against their fellow Jews who held rallies when they were being slaughtered!"

I took out my pocket watch to check the time.

"Why look at that nasty little thing?" my cousin asked.

I smiled and said, "Is it so nasty, then?"

"Yes," she said. "Isn't it? When is the time it tells ever a good one?"

I nodded and said, "That's true, my dear. The times are bad. And now I'll be on my way, because I have a train to catch."

"Where are you going?"

"To Berlin."

"Berlin," she repeated sadly.

I nodded again. "Yes, Malka, my dear. I'm off to Berlin."

"What a terrible place Berlin is," Malka said. "All the bad things come from there."

"There are bad things everywhere," I told her. "Not just in Berlin."

"Do you have enough to eat there?" she asked.

"Malka," I said, "doesn't the Bible say man does not live by bread alone?"

"Finish the verse," she said. "'But from everything that is the word of God doth man live.' Where is the word of God in Berlin?"

"I see you haven't forgotten your Bible," I told her.

"You can spare me your compliments," she said. "I've forgotten something more important."

"What is that?"

She looked around without answering. I could see she was looking for something to eat that I could take with me. Bustling about her kitchen, she offered me every can of food she found. I laughed and said, "What am I going to do with so many cans? I have all I need."

All at once her face lit up. "How could I not have thought of it!" she exclaimed. "How could I not have thought of it!"

"Thought of what, Malka?" I asked.

She jumped to her feet with a youthful spryness, ran off, and came back with a goose liver. Goose livers, mind you, are not easily come by, especially in wartime. Although I had no idea what I was going to do with it, I couldn't bring myself to tell her that I was a vegetarian, since she was giving it to me from the goodness of her heart. Thrilled to have found a suitable gift, she wrapped it in paper and said, "Enjoy it! If you weren't in such a hurry, I'd roast it for you right now."

"I really must go, Malka," I said. "Please don't bother to walk me. I'll find the way myself."

She ignored me and set out by my side, lavishing good wishes on me and accompanying each wish with advice on how to make it come true. We walked until Brigitta Schimmermann's nursing home came into sight. "I'd better turn back before Frau Schimmermann sees me in my house smock," Malka said in alarm. We turned around and I walked her part of the way back.

"You haven't asked me what I was doing with a goose liver," she said as we were about to part.

"No," I said. "But I did ask myself."

Malka said, "Well, since you asked, I'll tell you. I had two lovely, fat geese that I was keeping for the day my son and husband came home from the war. One morning I went to feed them and found only one. 'Where's your partner?' I asked the other. It flapped its wings and said, 'Quack, quack,' as though it understood my question, but I didn't understand its answer. In the end, I solved the riddle on my own. Frau Schimmermann had hired some musicians to play for her soldiers, and they had helped themselves to one of my geese and left the other for me. Just as I was thinking that I had better slaughter that one, too, before someone else made off with it, who turns up but Alter Lipa Elbricht, the slaughterer from Leipzig, and does the honors. I'm sending half the goose to my husband and half to my son, and the liver is for you. The German officers like to give their families gifts from the battleground. Thank God we're Jews and not officers, and we give the battleground gifts. That's the story of the goose."

There I was, a man carrying a liver he had no use for. Although any meat eater might have envied me, my situation was far from enviable, since the liver was dripping all over me. Soon dogs scented the blood and began to chase me. I threw a stone at them and they ran off.

I walked on, thinking about the liver and me. I had to admit it was strange for a man to put himself to so much trouble to hold on to something he didn't want. Yet how much trouble was I prepared for? Driving away one pack of dogs was no guarantee there wouldn't be others. And on the other hand, how could I throw the dogs a liver that my cousin had lovingly deprived her son, her husband, and herself of for my sake? If only I could find the Russian prisoner, I'd let him have it and make him a happy man.

The wrapping was soaked through. I looked for a large leaf, but the gardens by the roadside had only small shrubs and flowers. My clothes were spattered with blood. I took out my handkerchief, tied it around the liver, and walked on.

By now, though, I was no longer thinking about the liver. I wasn't even thinking about my cousin Malka, or about anything that had happened since leaving Berlin. All I could think of was returning to my room in Frau Trotzmüller's boarding house and collapsing on its bed. Although it may not have been paradise, it was a sight better than being a homeless vagrant. The knowledge that I had a room to return to came as a relief, and I headed for the nursing home to say goodbye to Brigitta Schimmermann before continuing to the train station.

Lost in thought, I must have strayed from the path. Yet I couldn't have gone far from it, because I soon ran into a soldier from Brigitta's nursing home. I knew at once it was the golem she had told me about. The only difference was that the famous Golem of Prague was made of clay while this golem was made of skin and bones. Moreover, the Golem of Prague did what it was told to do and this golem couldn't be told to do anything, having lost its hearing and its other senses, so that there was no talking to it even in sign language. I took this to be a sign that the nursing home was near.

There were other indications that I was getting closer. For example, the soldiers' voices that I heard, singing the popular jingles of the day with their verses about the stalwart sons of Germany against whom the perfidious English, the swinish Russians, the execrable French, the odious Italians, and the slovenly Slavs had gone to war and would be crushed to a pulp.

All around me were gardens with flowers and winding paths. The liver dripped and pulsed in my hand and I had to grip it tightly to keep from dropping it. As I was looking for a shortcut to the nursing home, there, blocking my way, was the golem again. "Do you like liver?" I asked him, holding out my handkerchief. "Here, here's a goose liver. It's still alive. Take it, my friend. It's yours. Ask the cook to roast it and enjoy it. When did you last taste goose liver? You can't remember? Have some and you will."

Wishing to part on the best of terms, I declared:

"Soldier, let's be friends. You fought in the Kaiser's war. But we're all soldiers in one war or another. It's just that not all of us know which powers we're fighting for. You, my friend, have seen war's horrors. Now you're recovering from them. When you're better you'll go home and your loved ones will rejoice—your father, your mother, your brothers and sisters, your fiancée. I'm sure she must be beautiful, with blond hair and blue eyes."

I stood there, prattling away. Although I couldn't tell whether he understood me, it did me good to talk to him. There's something to be said for conversing with an idiot. You can say what you want without fear of sounding foolish.

My last words to him were:

"I'll say good-bye now and be off. You, too, must have somewhere to go. And since we'll never see each other again, we can part as friends and be sure we won't get in each other's way. Most of the world's problems come from Herr Schiller thinking that Herr Miller wants something from him. But if Schiller goes one way and Miller goes another, there's nothing to worry about. How do you plan to eat your liver, my friend, grilled or roasted? I wonder which you like better. Well, *ye'erav lekha, yevusam lekha*, as we Hebrews say in Hebrew. How do you Germans say it in German? When you see someone eating, you say *schmeckts*, don't you? Different peoples, different customs. Different languages, different expressions. And now I'll really say good-bye, because it's unlikely we'll ever meet again and you wouldn't recognize me if we did. Once you've been to war and seen so much killing and being killed, what can a plain good-bye mean to you?"

Chapter five

With a load off my hands and off my mind, I reached the nursing home. Brigitta saw my blood-stained clothes and took fright, thinking I had been in an accident. When I told her what had happened, she laughed and called for a servant girl to clean my jacket. Then, without waiting, she took a sponge and soapy water and set to work herself, squinting with satisfaction at each stain she removed. As she worked, she reminisced about the days in which I had been her costume adviser. All kinds of things I had forgotten, she still remembered.

"You never told me what made you become a historian of clothing," she said.

"If I could choose again," I said, "I wouldn't do it."

"But you did do it," Brigitta said. "Tell me why."

"I was young then," I said. "Before I could write about people from the past, I thought I had to picture them. And to do that I had to dress them in the clothing they wore in the times and places in which they lived. It turned out to be a hopeless task. My manuscript is so moth-eaten that all the mothballs in the world couldn't save it."

We talked on and on. I answered all Brigitta's questions and went off on some tangents of my own, the way you do to keep a conversation going with someone who is dear to you.

"Do you remember the time," asked Brigitta, "when I wanted to see that film in which I starred as the old king's daughter? We went to a movie theater and I was recognized, and the audience began to shout like madmen: 'She's here, the princess is here!'"

"Brigitta, my dearest," I said, "how could I forget? You launched a new fashion that night."

"I did?" Brigitta said. "I can't imagine what it was."

"If you've forgotten," I said, "I haven't."

"Tell me everything, darling," said Brigitta.

Although I knew very well that Brigitta Schimmermann never forgot anything, I was happy to comply. "How can you not remember?" I asked. "Everyone in the audience wanted a keepsake from the most beautiful actress in Berlin and started to rip your outfit apart. I had to drape my overcoat around you to keep you from being stripped naked."

She laughed her enchanting laugh and said, "I can't believe I forgot the whole thing. If you hadn't reminded me, I could have lived my whole life without recalling it. But you still haven't told me what fashion I launched."

"When everyone saw the fabulous Brigitta Schimmermann in a man's overcoat," I said, "men's coats on women became the rage."

"It's amazing how it slipped my mind," said Brigitta.

"That's only because your mind knew it could depend on mine," I said.

"Who knows what else you may know about me that I don't," she mused.

"In that respect," I said, "you're no different from the rest of us. We never know about ourselves what others do. And that's even truer of you, Brigitta, my dear, because you're too busy taking care of others to have time to think about yourself."

"And you?"

"Me? I'm forced to think about myself all the time."

"How come?"

"Because I'm too intimidated by others to think about them. And since a man has to think about something, that leaves me."

"You must know yourself very well then," said Brigitta.

"That's just it," I said. "The more a person thinks about himself, the less he knows himself. And since such a person is of no great interest to anyone, let's talk about someone else."

"I'm sure you're right about him," Brigitta said. "But since you've mentioned him, I'm curious."

I said, "Such a person could never satisfy your curiosity. He might think about himself constantly, but he couldn't tell you what he thought under pain of a whipping. And to tell you the truth, Brigitta, I'm annoyed at him for bothering you with such foolishness. I wish the telephone would ring right now with news that the entire general staff was on its way to visit your nursing home."

"But why?" Brigitta asked.

"So that this conversation might end," I said.

"You don't need the general staff to end it," said Brigitta.

Yet not only did she not end the conversation, she didn't pick up the telephone when it rang. And when it rang a second time she said into the receiver, "I'm busy," turned back to me with a smile, and said:

"And now tell me what you've learned from all your thinking."

"If that's an order," I said, "I suppose I'll have to obey it."

She gave me a fondly intrigued look. There's nothing like being thought intriguing to get a man like me to speak, and once I began, my words ran on by themselves. For your sakes, I'll be brief and give you the gist of them.

The story is told of a man who was directed to go to a certain place. On his way, he encountered a mountain. If I go around it, he thought, I'll lose time, so I had better climb over it. Yet reaching what he took to be the mountaintop, he saw it was but the first of many peaks. He kept on climbing, and the more he climbed, the more peaks he reached, one after another, until there were seven in all. At the top of the last peak, he saw a huge rock. A rock like this, he thought, must be here for a reason. Something valuable is surely hidden beneath it. I'll go no further until I've moved it and seen what that is.

And so the man labored to move the rock. He worked at it one day, and a second and a third, until seven days had gone by. Yet when he finally managed to move the rock, there was another rock beneath it. He moved that one too, and beneath it was another rock, seven rocks altogether, each of which took seven days to move. When the seventh rock was rolled aside, he saw a cave. A cave concealed by so many rocks must have a great treasure in it, he thought. I had better see what that is.

The cave was barred by a door with seven locks. After breaking each lock, the man opened the door. Behind it was a second door, and then a third, and a fourth, and a fifth, and a sixth, and a seventh, each with seven more locks. He broke lock after lock and opened door after door until the last door was opened. Beyond it was an ascent with seven levels, each level taking seven days to cross. When he had crossed the last of them, he came to another cave. This one, too, had seven doors, and seven locks on each door, and seven levels taking seven days to cross. And after it came still another cave, followed by yet another.

Inside the seventh and last cave, the man found a large barrel. Certain that the treasure guarded by so many mountains, rocks, and caves must be in the barrel, he pried it open. In it was a second barrel, and in that a third, seven barrels one after the other. Prying the last of them open, he found a box sealed with seven seals. He broke all seven and found another box, followed by another and another, and each time he felt sure that this box was the last. And although the seals were made of wax, and wax is a soft substance, each seal took him seven days to break, not because his hands were weary, but because the wax was dry and crumbly, so that the more of it fell off, the more remained.

Inside the seventh box was something in a wrapper. The man tore off the wrapper and uncovered a corked flask. He uncorked it with his teeth and pulled out many scrolls, each scroll inside another flask, and each flask in another wrapper, and each wrapper tied with another ribbon. I can't tell you whether there were seventy-seven of them or more, because he was in too much of a hurry to count. When he had untied all the ribbons, and torn off all the wrappers, and opened all the flasks, and pieced together all the scrolls, a smaller scroll fell out of them. To make a long story short, just as there had been seven mountains, one above another, and seven caves, one inside another, and seven doors and seven levels and seven barrels and seven boxes, seven tiny scrolls now fell out of the small scroll, each tinier than the one before. The man opened them all until he came to the last and tiniest of them. On it was written:

"Fool! What did you lose here that made you come back to look for it?"

Brigitta laughed. Then she laughed again. The parable was so long that she had lost track of its point, or perhaps vice versa. "You've tried my patience, my dear," she said. "For that you deserve to be punished. The worst punishment I can think of is making you spend another day here. My husband and father-in-law are arriving on the evening train. You must have heard many things about my father-in-law, not all of them complimentary. When you meet him you'll see that being detested by the socialists doesn't necessarily make you detestable. Not if you're my father-in-law, anyway. I'll let you in on a secret. I'm adding a wing to the nursing home, and Simon Gabel has drawn up the plans. I'm glad to say that that barbarian has actually listened to me and taken my wishes into account, and I have a feeling that my father-in-law will help with the financing. Stay another day and the four of us will spend a lovely evening together."

Schimmermann senior was known to me only by hearsay and from the photographs and caricatures of him in the newspapers. That evening I was introduced to him in person. A quick mind and ready conversationalist, he was also a big eater, drinker, and smoker whose cigar never left his mouth after dinner. At first he talked about the 1870 Franco-Prussian War, which was an idyll compared to the current war. Then he proceeded to the subject of German science, whose military contributions were greater than your ordinary German philistine thought. Not only were German researchers responsible for many inventions now aiding Germany's war effort, they had played a crucial role back in 1870, too. Their work on France in those years revealed that country's secrets and was an invaluable guide for the German army, just as their knowledge of French history and culture helped Germany formulate the war claims to which the defeated French were forced to agree.

From the lessons of the Franco-Prussian War, old man Schimmerman went on to his own experiences. "I was a young officer then," he related. "One day a group of us was summoned to the home of Flaubert, who had fled because of the fighting. Although he had a large collection of paintings and *objets d'art*, we left it all untouched to show our respect for him."

He looked a bit like Flaubert himself. The good food and ready conversation caused Brigitta to glow with pleasure, as did her raconteur of a father-in-law. He was in an expansive mood—and the more expansive he was, the greater his liberality, which Brigitta was in need of. New wounded kept arriving every day; her nursing home was full, and she wished to build a separate wing for convalescents awaiting medical treatment in Berlin. Although her operating expenses were covered by her husband, only her father-in-law could afford such a project, for which Simon Gabel had drawn up the plans.

It was midnight when Gerhard Schimmermann walked me back to my room. On our way he spoke in praise of Simon Gabel, whose contemporary architecture expressed the martial spirit of his generation, so unlike the pastoral nature of the pre-war period. It was men like Gabel who would build the new world, etc., etc. As far as I could see, two things were on Schimmermann's mind. The first was to show me that he didn't have an anti-Semitic bone in his body, Simon Gabel being a Jew. The second was to prove that you could build the new world without socialism. He was still talking when we reached my room. After checking to see I had everything I needed, he thanked me for having made Brigitta a happy woman by visiting her nursing home. Nothing pleased her more than knowing it was appreciated.

At that time I hadn't yet met Simon Gabel, whose reputation had spread throughout Germany. There were different opinions of him. Some considered him a great modernist who had dealt a death blow to the stultified architecture of the past by inventing a new contemporary idiom, and some thought him the evil genie of a nouveau-riche class that, lacking all confidence in its own aesthetic judgments, was in thrall to the pretentiousness of self-proclaimed masters. I had no firm view of my own. The only house of Gabel's I had been in, designed for a couple I knew, had a coldness despite its central heating and was far from the cozy home they had exchanged for it. And yet they professed to be delighted with it and swore by its efficient layout, in which there wasn't an unnecessary inch of space.

That night I picked up a book of Chinese legends that was lying on the night table by my bed. In it was a story about a venerable architect much loved by the emperor for designing palaces, castles, temples, and fortresses more beautiful than any built before. One day the emperor commissioned this architect to construct a new castle. Yet years went by and nothing was done, for the architect had lost all interest in working in wood and stone. Finally, prodded to execute his commission, he took a large canvas, painted a castle on it so skillfully that it looked real, and sent the emperor a message that the task was completed. The emperor came and was ecstatic, having never seen such a magnificent castle in his life. Soon, however, word reached him that it was nothing but a painting. Furious, he summoned the architect and said: "I made you the chief builder of my realm and trusted you unconditionally. Is this how you repay me?" "But what have I done?" asked the nonplussed architect. "What have you done?" scolded the emperor. "Not only have you disobeyed my orders, you have deceived me into thinking that the mere appearance of a building is a building." "Mere appearance, you say?" replied the architect, knocking on a door he had painted. "We shall see about that." The door opened and the architect stepped through it and was never seen again.

This story made a great impression on the angel of dreams—who, however, got it all backwards. All night long he built house after house and took me to see every one of them. Yet whichever I sought to enter, the door slammed in my face. In the end, the houses, too, turned into doors. I opened one door and found a second behind it, and another behind that, seven doors in all, until I was exhausted and on the verge of despair. Just then an automobile drove by. In it was Simon Gabel. Although I was surprised to have recognized him, never having seen him before, I was puzzled by his failure to offer a tired man like me a ride.

I had finished eating breakfast by myself when Brigitta appeared, dressed in a traveling outfit. It seemed that Simon Gabel had arrived that morning for the opening of a new hospital designed by him near Lunenfeld and had invited Brigitta, her husband, and her father-in-law to attend. She was just returning from the event after parting from the two Schimmermanns, pleased that the new wing of her nursing home would resemble a smaller version of Gabel's structure. It would house the wounded for whom it would be a first stop before being sent to a hospital or to the professors in Berlin, who were eager to learn about new kinds of injuries unfamiliar to them from peacetime. Indeed, a detachment of casualties was setting out for Berlin that evening and Brigitta convinced me to wait for it, since her head nurse, Bernhardina, was accompanying it and would see to all my travel arrangements.

Though she was busy preparing this detachment and selecting its members, Brigitta found time to tell me about some of the strange cases that she had seen or heard of from reliable sources. For example, there was the soldier who was so lightly wounded that it was hardly worth wasting a bandage on him. Nevertheless, a doctor took a liking to him and put him down for several days of convalescence. On his way, his train crashed into another train. Most of the passengers were killed instantly and the soldier died of his injuries.

From the physical cases, Brigitta proceeded to the mental ones. There were perfectly healthy men who ate and drank and had nothing visibly wrong with them, yet were mindless. The golem, for instance: just picture a normal body without a brain. "Since the day he arrived," Brigitta said, "we haven't been able to get a word out of him. He can't remember his own name, or where he comes from, or the slightest clue to his identity. He was found in a pile of mangled bodies on the battlefield, the only survivor in his company. But I have to go now. I'm afraid I won't see you again before you leave. Have a good trip, darling. If you're ever in Leipzig again, do give me a ring. Now that you know where The Lion's Den is, it will be easy to find me. But I haven't even asked you about your trip to Grimma! Did you get to see Dr. Levi's widow? Poor Levi is dead and his widow hasn't long to live. What will happen to all his books? And what about Mittel? Men write books and collect them and leave them to those who have no need of them. By the way, how is your own book coming along? It must have doubled in size from all the new army uniforms. Adieu, my dear."

As there were still a few hours left to departure time, I went to see my cousin again. She couldn't believe her eyes. Although I had promised to come back some day, who had ever heard of promises being kept so promptly in times like these? She was so delighted she didn't know what to do first.

We sat and talked. Or rather, she did all the talking—but since I sat and listened, it was still a conversation. She had sent the goose to the front in two packages, one to her husband and one to her son. In each was a note that said, "In case you're wondering why this goose has no liver, I gave it to a cousin of ours who turned up like a gift from heaven." Malka looked at me with tears of love and said, "You did a great thing, cousin, by coming to see me. And not only for me, but for my husband and son, because now I have news to write them. Until now every letter was full of the same old things. How many times can you say, 'I haven't found an electrician yet,' or 'There's still no cooking gas,' or 'Whenever it rains the house is flooded,' or 'The workers all do such shoddy jobs'? Now my husband and son will have something to read about, all because of you."

We talked until it was time to say good-bye.

I returned to the nursing home and waited for the soldiers to set out. There was a great commotion, as there always is when troops are on the move. The entire staff was on hand to help; wherever I turned, I was in somebody's frantic way. Although I caught a glimpse of Brigitta, I didn't approach her, not wanting to distract her when she needed every minute. She was truly a wonder, Brigitta. No matter how pressing her business, she never looked flustered.

A nurse came to tell me that the departure was delayed and we would be taking the night train. It was a pity I hadn't known earlier, because then I could have spent more time at my cousin's and let her talk to her heart's content. My surprise visit had done her a world of good, a Jewish woman alone among Germans who made her feel like a stranger, at the very moment that her husband and son were risking their lives for Germany. Not that I still couldn't have gone back to see her and returned in time for the night train, but I was afraid so much excitement would be bad for her.

I walked up and down the courtyard, thinking. Was there a reason that Brigitta Schimmermann had forgotten to tell me where to meet for lunch? Or that I couldn't find The Lion's Den when I was looking for it and found it when I wasn't? Or that Brigitta wasn't in Leipzig that day, causing me to take the train to Lunenfeld? Now that I was in Lunenfeld, I wanted only to return to Berlin, although all I had wanted in Berlin was to be somewhere else. Then again, I was returning to Berlin because my hopes of being elsewhere had been dashed.

To take my mind off aggravating thoughts, I tried thinking of other things. At first I concentrated on Hebrew roots again, as I had done that sleepless night in Grimma. Then I thought of Dr. Levi and of his quarrel with the Reverend Rabbi Gesetztreu and Herr Hochmute. Dr. Levi was no longer in this world and his estate was in a sorry state. What would become of his books? Were they really doomed either to fall into the hands of unscrupulous dealers or to be eaten by mice?

I put Levi and his estate aside and thought of collectors and bibliographers, such as Mittel, who had a house full of Hebrew books and an only son who couldn't read Hebrew. Now Mittel's son was fighting against Russia, which Mittel had fled because of the police, who had become no better in Germany.

But why dwell on Mittel and his son when a man could think about himself? Once there was a Jew who lived in the Land of Israel and lacked nothing. Nevertheless, the notion got into him to live abroad. And so he traveled to Germany and rented a room in its capital, where he was free to do as he pleased so long as the police had no objection. But while life in Germany may have been good before the war, there was nothing good about it now. I've already mentioned that my room was too small and my clothes were too heavy; it's time

I also told you about Mondays and Thursdays, on every one of which I had to report to my draft board in Tempelhof. For the time being, I had a deferment. Yet while this satisfied the draft board, it didn't satisfy the average German, who assumed that anyone not a cripple was a draft dodger. Even though the greatest German patriot no longer wished he were at the front, plenty of Germans wished I were, as I indeed soon would be if the war went on. And since a soldier at the front could expect either to die, be wounded, or take sick, I would end up, if alive, in a hospital or a nursing home. Perhaps the nursing home would be Brigitta Schimmermann's, in which I was now a guest.

But why worry about the distant future when there was a closer one? In an hour or two, I would be on my way to Berlin. What awaited me there? A cramped room. At the same time, however, I had to admit that no one in Berlin had ever done me the slightest harm, and that Frau Trotzmüller's dream had made her and her daughters think well of me and regret my leaving, since as long as I boarded with them there was hope for young Trotzmüller's return. Now that I would be back again, they would have their hope back, too.

I was still in the courtyard when Brigitta appeared, holding her handbag. As charming and beautiful as ever, she smiled at me warmly and said: "I'm sorry to have been such a poor hostess. And most of all, I'm sorry I didn't put every minute you were here to better use. But institutions have their responsibilities. Not that I don't have a good, dependable staff, especially our head doctor, who is one of Germany's leading and most innovative psychiatrists. Still, nothing gets done if I don't do it myself. And now, darling, let's have a cup of tea. If you'd like, I'll tell you about my soldiers and their traumas."

Brigitta brought me to her room and tea was served. We drank and talked. Once or twice the telephone rang and was ignored by her, and when somebody knocked on the door, she called, "If it's not urgent, please don't bother me." The day grew dark and the electric lights came on. Had the furnishings not been so shabby, I could have sworn I was back in Brigitta's old place in Berlin, before she married Gerhard Schimmermann and took up charity work. All my troubles since setting out for Grimma were forgotten. Even though

I had accomplished nothing in the matter of Dr. Levi's books, it was worth it all just to be with Brigitta again, as in the old days when she was the idol of Berlin.

Brigitta picked up a folder and said, "These are drawings done by soldiers in our care." She opened the folder and showed me a drawing of a nightmare, another of a pornographic scene, and another of a little girl leading a muzzled goose by a rope. Then she took out a drawing of a strapping young man captioned "Golem." This was a term people knew in those days because a German author had written a book about the Golem of Prague that was widely advertised by his publishers in the hope of earning back the prodigal advance paid him. As a publicity stunt, they even assembled a group of invalids, arranged them according to height, and gave them flash cards to hold that spelled "G-O-L-E-M." Paraded through the streets of Leipzig during the annual fair, when the city was crowded with visitors, this human billboard made "Golem" a household word. Everyone knew all about the Prague Golem, who was made of clay and brought to life by a parchment placed beneath his tongue with the sacred name of God on it. "Tonight," Brigitta said, "I'm sending the professors a golem of flesh and blood with nothing beneath his tongue but his chin. I must have told you he was found on the battlefield in a pile of corpses. Now he's off to Berlin with the others. The professors can't wait to get their hands on him. Here, darling, let me pour you another cup. If you'd like, I can tell you lots more."

But before she could pour me more tea, the telephone rang with urgent business. Brigitta bade me farewell and left the room. Not wanting to remain by myself, I left too.

Chapter six

We set out on the night train. The station was sunk in darkness and the light in the train was dim. The benches and floor were filthy. Although it was raining heavily, the windows couldn't be closed because of the same missing straps that had prevented them from being opened on the train to Leipzig. Opposites, so it seemed, could have the same cause. Nor did the open windows keep the train from stinking of cheap tobacco, as the rain outside formed a solid wall and the humidity inside made the dampness even damper.

If the trip back to Berlin was nonetheless better than the one leaving it, this was only because of Sister Bernhardina and her soldiers, who did their best to be helpful. Yet the closer we came to Berlin, the more anxious I grew. Not only had I not found another room, I couldn't count on getting my old one back. Berlin was full of refugees, no new housing was under construction, and empty rooms were grabbed in no time.

The soldiers rolled dice and told dirty jokes while Bernhardina dozed off and I sat thinking. Although I'm not a man for grand notions, I couldn't help reflecting what a jest of Fate it was to make me take so many trains to get from Berlin to Berlin. Just then there was a roar of laughter. One of the soldiers had told a joke and even Bernhardina woke up and laughed. She must have known from the guffaws what joke it was. In the entire car, there were only two of us who didn't join in.

The second man was the soldier I had given my cousin's goose liver to. There wasn't a flicker of life in his blank face. Brigitta should never have called him a golem. He wasn't worthy of the name, because the Golem of Prague was more human. Imagine a long pair of arms, a long pair of legs, a face like dried mud, a dead, witless stare, and an immovable head on two sunken shoulders. What could a creature like that understand, much less do if commanded?

I felt the golem staring at me. Did he remember me and the liver? I thought of my cousin and her family, who had gone without the liver for my sake, and of the dogs that had chased me for it, and of the Russian prisoner I had wanted to have it, and of giving it to the golem instead. If I asked him whether he had enjoyed it, what answer could I hope to get?

I pictured the Russian prisoner, standing in a foreign field. It surprised me, not only that Brigitta hadn't taken him in, but that she had felt no pity for him and had scolded me because I had. The thought of him made me forget where I was. "Young man," I told him, "don't count on me to help, but I'll be glad to listen to whatever you have to say. You'll feel better once you get it off your chest. What's bothering you? Tell me, my friend, tell me. You needn't be shy. If I interrupt you, it's not from impatience but only to let you know I'm paying attention. Why are you looking at me like that? I'm speaking a language you don't understand because I want to get you to talk. How old are you? Not even twenty, I'll bet. How old could you have been when you went to war? Perhaps eighteen. You thought you would fight for king and country and be a great hero and mow down the enemy, but before you could harm a hair on his head you were his prisoner. Now you've lost all interest in killing. You only want to go home to your mother and never hear the sounds of war again, isn't that so, my friend?"

The Russian nodded.

"And now," I went on, "you sleep in a pigsty and wonder why you don't hate the enemy at all. I suppose you might even love him if he let you. But don't imagine that he hates you. It's an abstraction that he hates. We, too, are an enemy that your people never saw or knew. Where there is war there is hatred, and we live in a world that loves to hate. Would you like to hear a story? Once upon a time there were some Jews from Galicia who came to earn a living in Leipzig because they couldn't make ends meet at home. Their fellow Galicians offered them hospitality and advice, helped set them up in business, and welcomed them in their synagogue. The newcomers were happy to have a Galician-style synagogue in Leipzig that relieved them of the need to pray with German Jews who looked down on them as foreigners. Although the God of Israel is one, the synagogues built in his honor are many. In short, since this isn't the time or place for a lecture on Jewish customs, the Jews from Galicia prayed in the Galician synagogue in Leipzig and felt at home there. And while this isn't the time for a lecture on Jewish prayer either, the God of Israel may be one and his people may be one, but the same can't be said of their prayers. Moreover, even though the newcomers prayed with their fellow Jews from the same prayer book all were raised on, they quarreled with them in the end. Do you think it had to do with money? Money had nothing to do with it. God gave them all their daily bread and none of them needed his neighbor's. No, it was over matters of principle. Although God is one and his Torah is one, Jews have many principles. And so they went and founded a new synagogue and named it for von Hindenburg to let their fellow Jews know they would deal with them as von Hindenburg dealt with his foes."

The Russian prisoner looked bewildered. He must have wondered how anyone could say so much in German when no German had spoken more than a few words to him since the day he was taken prisoner. As soon as I looked up, however, he and the field were gone. There was only the golem, staring at me. Was he still tasting the liver?

The lights of Berlin glowed on the horizon. Bernhardina brushed the sleep from her eyes, stretched, and told the soldiers to gather their gear. The soldiers put away their dice and began collecting their things while exclaiming, "Berlin, Berlin!" I felt too dejected to move. It was all I could do to take down my bags.

Bernhardina noticed this and said:

"The soldiers will bring your bags to your home."

A home, I thought, is exactly what I need. Not having one, however, the next best thing was my boarding house. Although it had no air, no light, no joy, no life, and no anything, it was the only place there was.

Berlin! The station was teeming with soldiers coming from all over and going everywhere. Germany was fighting a great war on many fronts. It was hard to say who was worse off, those coming or those going, but this wasn't the time to decide. I had to get to a boarding house in which I didn't know if I still was a boarder, because my room had most likely been rented and there wouldn't be another.

"If you'll write down your address," Bernhardina said to me, "I'll have your bags delivered."

I pulled myself together, took pencil and paper, and wrote the name of the boarding house with its street and number. Bernhardina read what I wrote, glanced at the soldiers, pointed to one of them, and said: "Take this gentleman's bags and bring them to his residence." The soldier took the piece of paper, read the address aloud, and reached for my bags.

It was then that a strange thing happened. The golem, who had been passive until now, snatched my bags from the soldier and blurted, "Me, me, me!" This was as worrisome as it was odd, because who knew what a golem might do with my bags or where he might bring them? Bernhardina, who had handled many troop transports without ever being challenged, was taken aback. Quickly, however, her expression changed from alarm to anger and she snapped:

"Put those bags down!"

The golem paid her no attention. "I'll call the police and have you locked up," she warned him. When this, too, had no effect, she tapped her head with her finger and said, "He's not all there."

What was to be done? Although no one could trust a golem who didn't know up from down, neither could my bags be pried loose from him, as he was hanging on to them for dear life while threatening to lower them on the head of whoever tried taking them away. In the end, after a brief consultation, it was decided to let him carry them with the first soldier as his escort. The golem, who couldn't have cared less whether he had an escort or not, began walking off with my bags. The soldiers sang:

> *Hanschen klein*
> *ging allein*
> *in die weite Welt hinein.*

I said good-bye to Bernhardina and the soldiers and went to obtain a residence permit from the police. Although I was a foreigner and the hour was late, I was asked no questions and given the permit. The only comment was the complaint of the desk sergeant, "You Austrians are never on time." Taking my leave of him, I walked to Fasanenstrasse.

Despite its being almost midnight, Berlin was wide awake. The streets were crowded, the streetcars were running, and the taxis, which were never available when you needed them, sped back and forth between the cabarets and the taverns. For every German who had gotten rich from the war, another cabaret or tavern had opened, and if you didn't bump into a man dressed as a woman every time you passed one of them, you bumped into a woman dressed as a man. Or else, if you managed to avoid both, you were clutched at by the lame and the blind and every species of invalid made by man or God. Between one cripple and the next, women held out their hands and asked for money or other favors.

As I neared Fasanenstrasse, the streets quieted down. All the houses were sleeping, to say nothing of the Reform temple, which slept from one Friday night to the next. You've timed things badly, I told myself. The boarding house has gone to bed and you'll have to ring and wake everyone. They say every delay is good in its way, but waiting to travel with Brigitta Schimmermann's legion of the wounded had nothing good about it. Brigitta had wanted to help and had only made things worse. Not that I would have minded so much were

I the sole victim—but now the entire boarding house would suffer, especially Frau Trotzmüller and her daughters. Even if Frau Trotzmüller was awake and grieving for her son, her daughters would not be and I would rob them of their sleep when I rang.

The three Trotzmüller girls, to whom I had never given a moment's thought while living with them under one roof, now appeared to me large as life. Stout, round Lotte, the eldest, peered up and lisped in her babyish voice, her head hunched between her shoulders. Before I could answer, there was her sister Hildegard, her wide eyes flashing sternly and a pitch-black curl I had never noticed bobbing up and down as she spoke, though the hard edge of her voice hardly needed its assistance. Next to her stood little Gert with her nose hidden in a field of red freckles above the open slit of her mouth. She must have forgotten to shut it in her annoyance at Hildegard for shushing her in the middle of a sentence.

Although I did my best to pay them no more attention than I had done when I was their boarder, they wouldn't go away. What, I wondered, gave them the power to be seen and heard blocks from their boarding house? It could only come from my guilt at having to wake them. Yet in the middle of trying to ignore them, it occurred to me that at least one of them must have stayed awake for me, since the golem's arrival with my bags would have warned them I was on my way. This realization caused me to slow down, there being no hurry if they knew I was coming. Which of the three sisters, I wondered, would be up? Not Hildegard. No one who could slight me for a cactus would give up a night's sleep for me now. If it was Lotte, on the other hand, her roundness might roll her back to sleep. And if it was Gert, Hildegard might sit up in bed and say, "Just look at her! Hatched yesterday and already chirping to wake the dead!"

And which of the boarders would wake first? Most likely it would be the official from the Tax Bureau, since wars cost money and money comes from taxes and the thought of all the taxes they had failed to collect kept tax officials up at night. Or perhaps it would be the couple from the war zone, who had heard the sounds of battle and were now alarmed by the slightest noise. And even if they slept through it, the servant girls would not. This would be a pity, because they worked hard to make the boarders happy and needed their sleep to get through the next day.

I should have taken to my heels and run in the other direction. But not only didn't I run, I felt too guilty even to walk. The whole street was sound asleep, each house in its fashion. The heavy stone houses slumbered dreamlessly; the dreams of the brick ones let in and shut out the world by turns. Above them rose the Reform temple with its gilded tiles made by the Wilhelm Kaiser Royal Tile Works. Once, the joke went, the Jews made bricks for Pharaoh and now the Kaiser made tiles for the Jews. Moreover, he made them of gold while Pharaoh's bricks were made of clay and straw.

It was midnight when I reached the boarding house. Just twenty-four hours ago Gerhard Schimmermann had walked me to my room and asked if I lacked anything. Now I was returning to a room that lacked everything. Every delay might be good in its way, but this one had nothing good about it.

Chapter seven

Given the hour, I was surprised to find the lights still on in the boarding house. I've said I'm not one for grand notions; it was clear the lights weren't for me. The only explanation I could think of was that one of the Trotzmüller girls had gotten engaged and was having a celebration—or else that Isolde Müller, the finishing school student, had invited her friends to a birthday party that was still going on.

Isolde Müller's parties always reminded me of a strange incident. One night I was lying in bed when Pharaoh's policemen arrived and buried me alive in the brick wall of a house. I groaned so loudly from within the bricks that God heard me and delivered me, putting me back to bed. Yet the policemen kept trying to choke me. I thrashed about and sent them sprawling except for the official from the Tax Bureau who lived across from me. Having drunk too much that night at Isolde Müller's party, he had mistaken my room for his own and crawled into bed with me, and now he was lying on top of me and crushing me.

No one answered when I rang the downstairs doorbell, so I pushed open the door and stepped inside. Although on any other night I would have been amazed to find the door unlocked after midnight, I was too pleased with my luck for amazement. Having surrendered the elevator key, I climbed the stairs. With every stair I climbed I heard the sounds of the boarding house more clearly. I was still debating how to explain my return to Frau Trotzmüller and her daughters when I reached the upstairs door. It, too, was unlocked. I had truly returned on a night of wonders: the same boarding house that went to sleep early all year long was now up and about with every door open. I was tiptoeing wearily to my room, hoping to steal off to bed unnoticed, when Hildegard barred my way, her eyes wide with tears.

"I'm back," I said.

She looked at me through her tears, took my hand, pressed it to her heart, and said, her eyes narrowing above her cheekbones: "So is Hanschen." And seeing that the name meant nothing to me, she added: "Ach, our poor brother! Ach, our poor brother!"

I squeezed her hand and tried to think of what to say, as you do when you know there must be something but can't imagine what it might be. Just then Lotte appeared. Peering up from a head hunched between her shoulders, she lisped the same news I had heard from Hildegard. "You can save yourself the trouble," Hildegard said, letting go of my hand and giving Lotte a stern look, "because I've already told him."

I shook Lotte's hand and told her how happy I was for her. She was still lisping away when Gert came to inform us that Hanschen was with their mother and that Frau Trotzmüller was crying. I shook Gert's hand and told her I was happy for her, too. Her freckles turned redder and her slit of a mouth grew pale.

The obvious thing to do, I thought, would be to go to Frau Trotzmüller's room and congratulate her and her son. On second thought, however, it seemed just as obvious to leave mother and son alone. It was all so obvious that I couldn't make up my mind, and meanwhile I was ready to collapse.

Obviously, there was no point in doing that. And so I stood asking myself, "How can you say nothing to the mother you heard sobbing every night for a son who has come home," and answering myself, "Why don't you just go to sleep," until Hildegard passed me in the hallway with her potted cactus and said, "This will look nice in Hanschen's room."

"But how did it happen?" I asked. "I mean, how did your brother come home? Did you have advance warning?"

Hildegard wiped away a tear. "How did it happen? Out of the blue. The doorbell rang and there was Hanschen. It's a good thing it was me who opened the door and went to tell Mother, because she would have passed out from sheer joy if it had been her."

Her own joy had turned Hildegard into a different person from the one who had slighted me for a cactus. I can't recall if her eyes were wide or narrow, but her voice was certainly choked. "I was sitting in my room," she said. "I wasn't sleepy and I went to get my knitting things. But I didn't feel like knitting either, and seeing that my bed wasn't made, I put down my needles to make it. Instead, though, I went to Mother's room. She was sitting on the couch with some photographs and she said, 'How will I recognize my boy when he comes home? He may have grown a beard or be wounded.' I said, 'Why would he grow a beard? He probably has a mustache like the Kaiser's.' Imagining Hanschen with a handlebar mustache made me laugh so hard that I couldn't stop. What a ridiculous thing for a little brother to have! I was in the middle of twirling imaginary whiskers when I heard voices. There were sounds below and the doorbell rang and rang. Mother said, 'Go open it,' and I said, 'Nobody has the right to disturb us at this time of night,' and she said, 'If you're not quick the whole boarding house will be woken.' By the time I realized she was right and went downstairs, the ringing had started again. Herr Schmidt from the Tax Bureau stuck his head out his door, and so did Isolde Müller from the big room, and so did all the other boarders. Mother started to apologize while I went to open the downstairs door in a fury. Two soldiers were standing there, one younger than the other. The first soldier asked, 'Is this the Trotzmüller boarding house? Sister Bernhardina has sent the bags of the gentleman who was visiting Frau Schimmermann.' I looked at them and at the bags and wished they'd go to the blazes. But they just went on standing there, so I said, 'You have a lot of nerve! I'm going to call the police and have you both arrested.' Just then the chambermaid saw the bags and said, 'Why, these belong to the gentleman from the little room!' I said, 'That can't be,' but a second later, *mein Herr*, I realized you must have returned and I said, 'Bring the bags inside and be off with you.' The soldiers brought in the bags and were about to go when Gert came downstairs and screamed, 'Hanschen!' We thought she had gone mad, but she kept screaming, 'Hanschen, Hanschen!' Then she turned to one of the soldiers and said, 'You're our brother Hans, tell me you're Hanschen! Mother, it's Hans, I swear to God!' And Hanschen, he didn't say a word, neither yes or no, and only stared at us. But I saw something change in his eyes, as though he was coming out of a trance—and then he whimpered and screamed, 'Mama!' And at that exact moment Mother screamed, 'Son!' I felt like screaming too, but I couldn't get a sound out. And the soldier who had come with Hanschen wouldn't leave him because he said he was responsible for returning him to Sister Bernhardina. Nothing could change his mind. I had to make phone calls to all kinds of high places to get him to agree."

I was on my last legs. But though it was time to go to bed, how do you cut short a sister who is telling you, not just about a brother, but about a brother who has returned from the dead? The clock struck one. The friends and family who came to welcome Hanschen had split into two groups. Those who lived nearby had gone home, and those who lived further off had stayed to sleep in the boarding house, the streetcars having stopped running. The building was silent. Whoever was gone was gone and whoever was in bed was in bed. It was so quiet you could hear them sleeping. I felt an ear-splitting yawn but was too exhausted to open my mouth to let it out. Before I could ask Hildegard about my room, she had gone to see if all the guests were taken care of.

Gert came along, saw me standing there, and began to tell me all about Hanschen. She told me what Hanschen was doing now, and where Hanschen had stood when she recognized him, and what her mother had said when she saw Hanschen, and how Hanschen's companion wouldn't leave Hanschen because he thought Hanschen should return to Hanschen's unit, so that if Hildegard hadn't made some telephone calls he would have taken Hanschen with him and there would have been no Hanschen. "We used to have dreams like that," she said, "in which we dreamed we saw Hanschen and woke up and Hanschen was gone." And Hanschen had gotten taller, so that the Hanschen who came home didn't look like the Hanschen who went to war. She, Gert, was the first to notice this; even her sisters admitted it. And Hanschen's face had changed and so had Hanschen's eyes. She didn't care if Herr Schmidt said eyes never changed, anyone could see that Hanschen's eyes were not the same.

Gert went on and on about Hanschen. You could tell how she worshiped him from the way she uttered his name. Her eyes kept filling with tears and her little nose reddened. By now I was literally falling off my feet. Not one of my five senses was still working. The only word of Gert's I could make out was Hanschen. I don't remember what made her stop or at what point she left me, but as soon as I saw that I was alone I headed for the little room that I had left three days before.

There was a gasp. I turned around and saw Gert staring at me in horror.

"What's wrong?" I asked.

She gasped again and said, "That's Hanschen's room. Hanschen has just gone to bed. He's asleep."

Her horror changed to entreaty. "If you step into Hanschen's room, *mein Herr*," she whispered, "you'll wake Hanschen."

In a word, my room was now Hanschen's and Hanschen was not to be disturbed. After all he had been through, he deserved a good night's sleep. Not that I deserved less after being on the road for so long, but you couldn't expect a foreigner to vie with a long-lost son.

I stood in the hallway, midway between Hanschen's room and the front door. At that moment the door opened and in walked an old woman, pulling an old man behind her. Gert threw her arms around them and sobbed while repeating all she had told me: how Hanschen had suddenly appeared, and how she had recognized Hanschen first, and how wonderful Hanschen was, and how good it was to have Hanschen back. Then she scolded her grandparents for traveling in the middle of the night. Hadn't Hildegard told them on the phone, "Don't come tonight, it's too far and there's no transportation"? And yet they hadn't thought of themselves and had only wanted to see Hanschen.

Dead tired from their travels, the old couple told Gert how they had changed from train to train and from streetcar to streetcar, and how they had had to walk in the end when the conductor informed them that the last streetcar had left. Now that they had finally arrived, they were too exhausted to rejoice in their grandson's return and wanted only to sleep.

Frau Trotzmüller appeared, saw her parents, and embraced them with more tears. Taking her father by one hand and her mother by the other, she led them to Hanschen's room and opened the door a crack to let them glimpse him lying in bed, making snuffling sounds with his face buried in the pillow. "He's asleep, he's asleep," she whispered.

The old couple nodded and said, "He's asleep." Frau Trotzmüller let them have her room and slipped quietly into Hanschen's, because there wasn't an empty bed in the boarding house. Before long everyone was asleep except me, the only one without a place to lay his head.

I stood looking at the doors of the rooms, which had dissolved into a magical tableau. The light in the hallway gleamed on the doorknobs, every one of which was locked. Twenty-four hours ago I had lain in a comfortable bed, reading a charming legend about an architect who walked through a door painted on canvas. Now I stood before the doors of real rooms and not one would open for me.

Hildegard passed by without noticing me. Before I could say a word, she had turned off the electricity except for a small night-light and gone to her room. I was left all alone in the hallway. At first I felt conspicuously large. Then I felt insignificantly small. Then I stood like a golem awaiting orders. There was no one to give them.

I leaned against a wall and tried to think. What was I supposed to do now? There was still the dining room, on whose carpet I could bed down for the night. I was about to stretch out on it when the door opened and in came the chambermaid, carrying blankets and pillows. Yet not only was I too tired to feel grateful for them, I didn't need them all, because two more servant girls soon arrived with more. Why so many? Because the dining room doubled at night as the staff's bedroom. Now that the boarding house was asleep, the staff had to sleep, too. That left me out in the cold.

Where was I to go? It was nearly two A.M. and all the hotels were shut for the night. And even if one were open, how would I know where it was, let alone have the strength to get there, much less hope to find a vacant room in it? It was wartime, Berlin was flooded with people, and every hotel had more guests than it could handle.

The servant girls made their beds and waited for me to leave so that they could turn in for the night. Yet while leaving was clearly the thing to do, I had no idea where to go. I glanced at the chambermaid, who had been tipped by me every week without ever being asked for a favor. She felt my eyes on her and said:

"It doesn't look like there's any room for you, *mein Herr.*"

"What do you suggest I do?" I asked.

She made a sound like a hiccup and said, "I really don't know what to tell you. The rooms are all taken. Even Herr Schmidt has had to share his room with someone, and you know, *mein Herr,* how difficult Herr Schmidt can be. We've worked extra hard tonight because of everyone who came to see Hanschen and now we have to get some sleep."

"You do indeed," I said. "I wouldn't want to deprive you of it."

The chambermaid sized me up like an undertaker measuring a corpse for its grave. What she said next, dear reader, was this:

"I suppose the bathroom won't be needed until the morning. I'll make a bed for you there."

Soon she returned and said:

"Your bed is ready."

I went to the bathroom, thinking she had set up a cot in it. She had done no such thing. In the bathtub were a folded rug, a pillow, and a blanket. Although I had heard of hotels putting guests up in bathtubs, I had never believed it was true. Now I knew better.

I was in no position to be choosy. I locked the bathroom door, undressed, and got into bed—that is, into the tub. I believe it was

Rabbi Nachman of Bratslav who said that God in His goodness conducts the world's affairs more splendidly from day to day. My own affairs were an exception. From day to day, they were conducted more squalidly.

Somehow I managed to fall asleep. The reason I know I did is that I had a dream. What did I dream? I dreamed that a great war had broken out and that I was called up to fight and took a solemn oath that if God brought me home safe and sound, I would sacrifice to Him whatever came forth from my house to greet me. I returned home safe and sound and behold, coming forth to greet me was myself.

Chapter eight

I was awoken by the rasp of a door and the grumble of a man. What had happened was that the man had found the bathroom door locked and forced it open, only to discover me lying in the tub in an unconventional state. This made him grumble, which woke me. I snatched my clothes, dressed, and made way for him without stopping to wash up.

The boarding house was still sleeping off the night's excitement. Only the staff was awake. When the dining room had been cleared of its mattresses, I opened a window and sat down to think. Then I went to wash. Someone else was now in the bathroom. I returned to the dining room and waited. When I tried the bathroom again, someone else was there.

I went to a café, drank a cup of what passed for coffee, and read a newspaper. Although the papers were full of Germany's victories, there were no celebrations in the streets. Not that Germans didn't believe what they read. They believed every word of it, since the press printed the communiqués of the General Staff and the General Staff never lied. It was just that everyone's private setbacks made the nation's triumphs look small.

I sat holding the newspaper with my empty cup in front of me. The newspaper was a hymn of praise to Germany. No other country was as mighty. Wherever Germany's soldiers thrust their lances, destruction and conquest followed close behind. The Germans were indeed a stubborn people. Once they started something, they saw it through. And having started a war, they weren't about to stop fighting and killing and trampling underfoot. You may be right, my dear Mittel, that Germany has lashed out at its enemies and harmed only itself, but so far the harm is skin-deep. And even if Germany loses its shirt, it will clothe itself in war loot and feed itself with plundered crops.

I sat thinking of the days before the war, which now seemed like a poetic idyll. Yet since the hexameters of an idyll are of equal length and there was little equality before the war, perhaps it was not as idyllic as all that.

I recalled the day the war broke out. I was walking in a far neighborhood of Berlin and saw crowds of people, some cheering and some looking puzzled. And in fact it was puzzling: an archduke and his wife go for a ride in their carriage, and before you know it they're dead and the bullets that killed them have gone forth and multiplied and are killing more and more people. Mittel was right: the war wouldn't end quickly. The Germans were stubborn. Once they started something, they saw it through.

The war had made it hard for me to concentrate. That's why I've kept jumping from one thing to another. From my room on Fasanenstrasse I skipped to my winter clothes, and from my winter clothes to Dr. Levi's library. I can't say I was of any help to Levi's widow, but I did help another woman whose son came home because of me and left me homeless. At first I wondered why Brigitta Schimmermann called her zombie a golem, since the Golem of Prague was almost human and did what it was commanded, whereas the zombie was incapable of understanding the simplest command. Yet in the end he understood well enough and turned me out of my room. And with whose help? With my own, the help of the man who belittled him.

I took the telephone book and copied the addresses of all the boarding houses listed. Then I wrote down all the rooms advertised for rent in the newspaper. Then I returned to Fasanenstrasse and changed into a fresh collar.

The boarding house was in a holiday mood and fragrant with flowers. Frau Trotzmüller was sitting in the dining room with her son, having breakfast. All of Hanschen's welcomers were there, as were Lotte, Hildegard, and Gert, each looking adoringly at her brother in her fashion. The servant girls, in festive, freshly starched aprons, were waiting on them.

I congratulated Frau Trotzmüller on her son's return and stayed to chat a bit with her guests. First I asked them about themselves and they answered me, and then they asked me about myself and I answered them, and then I rose and declared, "It's time I went to look for a room." I was sorry the moment I said it, because I didn't want to sound annoyed that Hanschen had returned. Luckily, neither Frau Trotzmüller nor her daughters paid me any heed, being too blissful to hear what was said to them.

Let's put aside the homecoming of Frau Trotzmüller's long-lost son, then, and turn to the son who lost his home. This person made the rounds of Berlin's boarding houses, looking for a room. On his way, he reflected on all the generations from Adam's to the present. If only he could dress them in the appropriate garb for their time, place, and station, they would make a fine sight. All around him were mindless crowds of human beings dressed in the latest fashions, which he was too preoccupied with finding a room to notice.

It was getting dark. I had trudged from street to street and boarding house to boarding house. Most of the rooms were already rented, and those that weren't hadn't been rented for good reasons. And not only wasn't there a room for me, the ground beneath me didn't want me either. If you think I'm exaggerating, let me tell you that I pounded the pavements of Willemsdorf and Charlottensburg and Hallensee without success—that's three large neighborhoods right there. I should never have postponed returning to Berlin because of Brigitta Schimmermann's soldiers. Had I taken an earlier train, I would have arrived at the Trotzmüllers' in plenty of time to get my room back. And if you ask, what about Frau Trotzmüller's dream, I hope you don't think I owed it to her to interpret it with a pound of my own flesh. I'm not a man for grand notions and it's not my job to run the world. Although Brigitta's intentions were good, no good came of them for me. Never keep anyone waiting. Look what happened in the Bible to the concubine at Gibeah. Her master was delayed in Bethlehem and thousands of Israelites perished because of it.

I went to dine at a vegetarian restaurant. In order to save on electricity and waitresses, the owner served his customers at a single table. Some of them looked as though they ate out regularly and others as though they had decided to splurge on a single meal, the only decent food in those days being in restaurants. They sat huddled together and I sat with them. But although there was one table, one electric bulb, and one bowl for us all, this was as far as our unity went, as each of us was in a world of his own. One man studied his plate, another his newspaper, another his bill. The only thing we had in common was that none of us had ever paid so much for so little.

As I was leaving, I ran into my old friend Peter Temper, who was in charge of the big cats at the zoo. Peter had an upset stomach and had sworn off meat for the day, and he was cross with me as normally healthy people can be when they're feeling out of sorts. This irritated me and I said, "You're acting like a teething baby."

"And you," Peter said, "have teeth like goat's udders from nibbling so much grass."

"At least I don't look like a goat the way you do," I answered him.

He fixed his steely blue eyes on me and said, "Come visit me at the zoo and we'll see who looks like a goat."

"I'm not visiting anyone who treats his friends like first-year zoology students just because he has indigestion," I said.

Peter saw I was annoyed and tried to be friendlier. "Do you know Hanging Pieters?" he asked.

Hanging Pieters was a distinguished lion brought from the German colonies in Africa and named for a governor known for his harsh treatment of the natives. "How come you mention him?" I asked.

"He's not well," Peter said.

"Admit it," I said. "You're only telling me about Hanging Pieters so that I'll think it's him that's worrying you and not your hypochondria."

He laid a hand on my shoulder and said, "After I eat I'll go home, have myself some jug juice, and wrap myself in a blanket and sweat it out."

This was Peter Temper's routine. Every night before bedtime, rain or shine, he took a flask of red wine, added cinnamon and cloves, brought it to a boil, drank it while hot, pulled a blanket up to his chin, and slept eight or nine hours at a stretch.

After we parted, I went to a café.

The café was packed. All through the war the cafés were crowded with people. The men came to be with other men, and the women came because their husbands had gone out and they didn't want to be left behind. New cafés opened daily and still there weren't enough. You had to push your way into them, and others pushed from behind while you were pushing. And once you were seated those standing in line eyed you as if you had stolen their seat, although they were only there because of you, since the whole point was not to be alone. Worse yet, the old waiters were in the army and the new ones were all cripples. And in case you doubted it, they wielded their trays as though they meant to cripple you.

I don't remember how I managed to find a place. I ordered a cup of what was supposed to be coffee, and when I finished it, I ordered a second cup to keep the standees from thinking I was clinging to my seat. Besides which, although it would have been only fair to let someone else have it, I had chanced to meet an old friend. I hadn't seen him since the war broke out—and now here he was, at the very table I had sat down at.

This friend had the same first and middle names that I did, which was uncommon, since they don't as a rule go together. As our mutual acquaintances addressed him by his middle name and me by my first name, we were never aware of this until one Sabbath in synagogue when we were both called up by our full names to the Torah. Perhaps this explains the closeness we had always felt.

The year before leaving for Palestine, I visited my friend's town and stayed with his family. The household, with its set and cheerfully obeyed routines, made an unforgettable impression on me. My friend's father, a learned, observant Jew with a special fondness for the commentaries of the rabbis and the poetic riddles of Ibn Ezra, was a well-liked man whose innocence was sometimes laughed at but never mocked. His wife, a large woman, ran the wholesale fabrics store that they owned. It was said that she not only knew which retailer buying on credit was about to declare bankruptcy and default on his debt, thus enabling her to collect it in time, but that she would then lend the money back to him in order to keep him in business.

My friend's two sisters were as naïve as their father and better-looking and less delicate than my friend, whose studies had ruined his constitution. This was why their mother had forbidden them an education, apart from enough Hebrew to read their prayers, a bit of arithmetic, and a reading and writing knowledge of German. It wasn't her concern for their faith that made her keep them away from books, but her worry for their health. My favorite in the family, however, was my friend's grandmother. The daughter of the great scholar Rabbi Shlomo Hurvitz, she had laid aside the ways of this world for those of the World to Come. More precisely, the ways of the World to Come had become her worldly ones.

During my years in Palestine, my friend was a university student in Vienna and Berlin. One day after returning to Berlin, I came across him in the Royal Library, and after that we kept in touch and sometimes met at the sort of places that people like us frequented; this continued until the war broke out, when he was drafted and I remained in Berlin. That's the short version of it. If some day I'm given the opportunity to write the longer one, I'll do so. His name was Shmuel Yosef Bach. Years later, when I revisited my native town in Galicia, in which there was a Daniel Bach, I asked him if they were related. He said he didn't know, but that considering that his father was named Yosef and his grandfather Shmuel, it stood to reason there was some connection.

My friend looked thin and haggard. Although his chest gleamed with enough medals for a war museum, his face was as ravaged as scorched earth. A frail intellectual cast onto the battlefield, he had fought like a hero and had been decorated by the generals. Now, the honors studding his uniform drew admiring glances, some of which were cast my way too, since we were clearly on the best of terms.

We sat marveling at how we had met by chance at a café table. Once we were over our amazement, each of us asked the other how he was. "What are you doing in Berlin?" I inquired.

"I have a few days' leave," Yosef Bach said.

"How is your father?" I asked him.

He looked at me and said nothing.

For a moment I sat in silence. Then I said, "I hope he's all right."

"When the Russians took our town," my friend recounted, "everyone fled except my father and my grandmother. My father stayed because he didn't think the Russians would harm anyone who didn't harm them, and my grandmother stayed because of the needy who needed her. My father never missed a day's prayer at the synagogue. That day he took his prayer shawl and tefillin and started out for the morning service as usual. My grandmother said to him, 'Why don't you pray at home today, there aren't any Jews left in town to pray with anyway,' and he answered, 'I can't change the habit of a lifetime.' On his way he met the Angel of Death. The Russian troops hadn't entered the town yet, so it must have been a Ukrainian peasant who had come to loot the synagogue and killed my father for fear of being reported. According to another version, this peasant was out bird hunting; he aimed at a dove in the synagogue's window and hit my father instead. Whoever told it that way was probably thinking of the story in the Talmud about the rabbi whose life was saved when his tefillin turned into doves and flew away with him. But the two stories aren't the same, because even if the dove in the window was my father's tefillin, it did nothing to save him."

To take his mind off his father, I asked about his mother. "She died on the road from Cracow to Vienna," he said. "She was fleeing the Russians like the rest of our town."

I asked about his sisters. He answered:

"The older one is gritting her teeth and raising her children like any other war widow. The younger one is waiting for her husband to come home from the front. And now, my friend, it's my turn to ask you something."

"Wait," I said. "I'm not done."

"Who else is there in my family to ask about?" he asked.

I said, "You may have forgotten your grandmother, but I haven't. How is she? With so much suffering, such a saintly soul must have her work cut out for her."

Once more he said nothing.

"You can tell me," I said.

"She was killed by a wild animal," said Yosef Bach.

"What do you mean?" I asked. "Like by a bear in the forest?"

"Bears and forests are in fairy tales," he said. "She was killed by a wild pig on her front steps. A Cossack grabbed her and did what he did. And now, my friend, since all my family is accounted for, my question to you is: When is the Royal Library open? Are the hours still nine-to-nine daily?"

"I'm afraid I can't tell you," I said. "I haven't been there since the war started."

"Why not?"

"I can't tell you that either."

Yosef Bach said nothing.

"Why do you ask about the library?" I asked.

"Why? I'm curious to know what's been published since I was called up."

"You can be sure there's been plenty," I told him. "We Jews are called the People of the Book, but every year Germany publishes half as many books as we've produced in our entire history. What field are you interested in these days?"

"What field? I'll let you in on a secret. I've started work on a book myself."

"When someone like you says he's started work on a book, it must already be finished. What is it about?"

"I'm thinking of giving it the catchy title of *Phenomological Taxonomy.*"

"*Phenomono*.... ?"

"The title is beside the point," my friend said. "Let me tell you how the idea came to me. I was lying in a trench when I had an experience I never had before, yet which gave me a strong sense of déjà vu. A while later it happened again; this time I wasn't sure if it was the first time or not, because it both seemed that it was and that it wasn't. A few days later, it happened a third time. By now I was certain that the past was repeating itself—and not just once, but over and over. This made me think about the phenomenon itself. What had caused my first déjà vu, and why did it take a second one to make me think that the first might be real? Was the first an illusion, or was it, too, a memory of something that had happened and been forgotten? And if so, was I looking at an infinite regression? Right now, my friend, I'm trying to classify all phenomena taxonomically—in other words, by their defining characteristics. If you'd like, we can call my book *On The Repetition of Things* rather than *Phenomenological Taxonomy*. But now tell me what's happening with your universal history of clothing."

"I cut it," I said.

"You did? Why?"

"I had to take a trip and I didn't want to carry a heavy manuscript, so I snipped off the margins."

Yosef Bach laughed and I joined him.

Nothing lasts forever, not even a conversation in a café. My friend had to go, and I rose from the table with him. After we parted, I stepped into another café. Although I shouldn't have taken a seat from someone who still hadn't found one, I had nowhere else in Berlin to go.

But this, too, didn't last forever. When closing time came, I had to get up and leave. On my way out I encountered a group of young Palestinians stranded in Berlin by the war. Some were university students and some had come to learn a trade. Most made a living, with varying degrees of success according to their social and linguistic aptitudes, from giving Hebrew lessons to young German Zionists.

One of the group, a short, stocky man I had never met before, was introduced to me as a sculptor named Druzi. It was the sort of name that left you guessing if it belonged to a Jew, a Syrian, or a Lebanese. He had big, sleepy eyes and a flat-footed gait, which came—so he was later to tell me—from being a barefoot shepherd when he was young. As for the group he was with, they were bound for a bakery that made rolls, which they planned to eat hot from the oven. This was something unheard-of in Berlin, where rolls were eaten, if at all, cold for breakfast.

"I'd love to come along but I can't," I said just in case anyone thought I had nowhere to spend the night.

"Why can't you?"

"I'm expected somewhere."

"Where?"

"At my boarding house."

"How come?"

"They promised to wait up for me."

"What for?"

"What for? So that I shouldn't have to ring the bell."

"But why should you have to ring the bell?"

"Because I forgot my key."

"So?"

"So I phoned and told them to wait. I don't want to keep them up all night."

My friends took me by the arm and whisked me away with them.

There we were, a tiny band of Palestinians in the big city of Berlin. We talked about the German military campaign, which was going from victory to victory, though no one knew when the war would end or what the world would be like when it did. From Germany, we moved on to Palestine. Thinking of Palestine made us forget the hot rolls. Soon everyone said good night and went home.

Druzi the sculptor wouldn't let me go. "Come with me, I have something to show you," he said.

"I can't," I said.

"Why not?"

"Didn't you hear me say I'm keeping somebody waiting?"

"And if you're keeping some German tart waiting," he said, "must you deny yourself a rare pleasure?"

"What sort of pleasure?"

"If you've ever been to Baalbek," he said, "you may have seen dawn break on its ancient statues, causing them to emerge from the darkness as though from the bowels of the earth. I propose to give you a taste of the same experience in my studio."

He steered me to a courtyard where we climbed a thousand-and-one stairs to a musty loft smelling of plaster, clay, tobacco, and chill blocks of stone. Switching on a light, he took out a bottle of brandy, poured us both a glass, and launched a disquisition on the merits of different pipe tobaccos. From there he changed the subject to the grand old café waiters from the days before the war, who would gladly give a needy artist a cheap loan. Next, he asked if I had ever noticed how, when you were dying to be introduced to someone, something always got in the way at the last moment. The more you wanted to meet them, the less you succeeded, while anyone else you met was an annoyance, having usurped the place of the only person who mattered.

In the middle of all this Druzi sat himself down on a slab of stone, placed the brandy bottle by his feet, surveyed his statues, and said:

"Listen, gang, if you want Brigitta Schimmermann to join you, ask this gentleman to put in a good word for me."

He reached for the bottle, poured us both another glass, and exclaimed:

"Here's to Brigitta Schimmermann!"

We raised our glasses and toasted Brigitta Schimmermann. As I drank I murmured to myself:

"To your health, Brigitta, because I wouldn't have had a place to spend the night without you."

The first light of dawn appeared in the window. The electric lights paled and the sculptures in the loft breathed a bone-chilling cold. Druzi took a strip of cloth, dipped it in water, and made a compress for a statue that had a headache. Then he made another for a second statue. When he was done, he broke out a new bottle of brandy, poured himself a glass, swallowed it in one gulp, and sat down. His head dropped to his chest and he fell asleep while pointing to his statues and saying, "Please, gang, let's have some quiet."

I rose to go. He felt me rise and awoke. "How can you go when you haven't seen a thing yet?" he said. "Wait and I'll show you."

I sat down. His head dropped back to his chest and he fell asleep again. I rose to go a second time. He felt me rise this time too, awoke once more, and asked, "Would that German tart make a good model?" When he fell asleep a third time, I slipped away.

Chapter nine

I won't dwell any more on sheer happenstance. The powers responsible for it may know what purpose it serves. I do not. It makes me think of the twilight matter that connects our dreams and dissipates as fast as it forms, leaving only the dreams with nothing between them. I'll put aside, then, whatever has no bearing on our story, such as my friend Yosef Bach's *On The Repetition of Things*, the hot rolls we never ate, and Druzi the sculptor, who sought to wangle an introduction to Brigitta Schimmermann, whose charm and beauty he had hoped to sculpt in marble. Having seen the two of us together, he thought I could get her to model for him, yet in the end he let me go without asking. And since I wasn't asked, I'll get back to the point.

The point is this: It's a big world with many countries, each with its cities, villages, houses, and rooms. Sometimes one person has many houses and sometimes many people share one room. Our story is about a man who had neither a country nor a room, having left the land he lived in and gone to live in another, where he lost even the four walls that he had.

This man went from neighborhood to neighborhood, street to street, and house to house. He knocked on many doors, each opened by a landlady who showed him a room. Sometimes he liked the room and not the landlady, and sometimes the landlady and not the room. Although this made him uncertain which was better, a good room or a good landlady, he went on looking. After a while he had seen so many rooms that his legs played tricks on him and brought him back to ones he had already been in. Seeing him return, the landlady was all smiles, certain he had decided to rent her room. Once she realized her mistake, she swore at him for wasting her time and he turned and slunk away. This made him so cautious that he shied away from houses in which perfectly good rooms were no doubt waiting for him. Moreover, his eyes and legs were at cross-purposes: what the former wished to look at, the latter refused to take him to, and what the latter wished to take him to, the former were too tired to look at. In the end, his legs grew heavy and his eyes began to shut. The minute they did, Berlin and its houses disappeared. As soon as that happened, Jaffa and its sand dunes took their place—the same Jaffa he had once had a room in.

This room was small, with a balcony. But while the balcony was also small, it had a big advantage, which was that it looked out on a garden in which grew lemons and other trees so magnificent that anyone hearing about them in Germany would have thought they belonged to a fairy tale. In their midst was a cistern whose water could be drunk and washed with and set out for the birds that sang outside the windows.

Having mentioned the windows, let me tell you about them. There were five. Two faced the street, and through them I saw right into the people who walked there. Another had a view of the valley in which the train ran to and from Jerusalem, so that whoever was aboard could see me and wave hello. I'd wave back, and the train being in no hurry, our two hellos met in flight. A fourth window looked out on the sea, the waters of God's great deep. From the fifth I saw the dunes of Jaffa, which were cinnamon-colored by day and peach-tinted by night. Sixty little houses dotted them and went by the name of Tel Aviv. I loved everyone in them, and they loved me, and God loved us all. Now God was angry, most of all at me for leaving his land, for which he had left me in the lurch. Yet even in his anger

I felt his love, since why else would he knock on my heart and call on me to return? Only I could not return, as there was a great war in the world, on land and on sea and in the air, and no way to travel to the Land of Israel. There was nothing to do but find a room in Berlin and live there until God made a path for me through the sea I once saw from my window.

Because of the hard times, not a few German Jews had started to take in boarders. Like most of my friends from Eastern Europe, I had made a point of not living with German Jews. They were more German than the Germans and didn't like our displaying our Jewishness, which led to arguments. Now, however, after a homeless night, I was less choosy. When I found a room in a Jewish home the next day, I took it.

The room was small and had all kinds of conditions attached to it. There were more rules and regulations than you might think would come with an entire house. Having no choice, I agreed to every one of them. As soon as possible, I promised myself, I would find another place with a less demanding landlord. Meanwhile, I brought my things from Frau Trotzmüller's and arranged them in the room. By the time I was done it was time for bed, and I lay down and fell fast asleep.

Before I knew it, the alarm rang and I awoke. I looked at the clock and saw I had better get up. Whether it was the bed, the previous day's exhaustion, or my night with Druzi, I hadn't slept so well in years—seven hours or more without waking. The only thing missing was some breakfast. All the landlord's rules and regulations hadn't included it.

I took my time thinking about where to eat. As hungry as I was, it was a treat to let my body lounge a bit longer, as it always is after a good night's sleep when all one's limbs are pleading for an encore and are grateful for any reprieve.

There was a knock on the door and the landlady entered. She wore a dark blue dress of thin wool that was neither new nor frayed, and her thick hair was piled high in what almost looked like a hairpiece. Wishing me a good morning, she asked if I was ready for my breakfast. There was no need to answer; my eyes spoke for themselves.

She went off and returned with a pot of tea, some toast, jam, and a newspaper. It was the last thing I expected; in attaching all their conditions, my landlords had neglected to tell me that breakfast was one of them. When I had eaten and drunk, my landlady returned to clear the dishes and said, "If that's enough for you to start the day with, I can bring it to you every morning." She paused and added, "And if you ask me, no one should have to spend his daytime hours in the same room he sleeps in at night. Come, I'll show you where you can sit during the day."

It was a spacious six-room apartment with furnishings such as you saw in well-off Jewish homes in Berlin. There was a room done in oak, and one in mahogany, and a living room in pear wood, and carpets and comfortable armchairs in every room. The chairs and carpets smelled of flowers and tobacco, and there were paintings on all the walls, some by well-known contemporary artists and some reproductions of the Old Masters, in addition to a wall-to-wall and floor-to-ceiling bookcase. When I came to know him, my landlord told me that he had grown up in a poor home and had no chance to get an education, but that he had begun to buy books for his pleasure as soon as he could afford them and continued to do so to this day.

I took a book from a shelf and read until lunchtime, when my landlord looked in on me to inquire whether I had slept well, and had I had enough breakfast, and was the book I was reading any good. A few days later he did this again. It was a Sunday and he had the day off from his business, and we began to talk and discovered we had mutual friends.

As we were talking, my landlord's wife appeared and suggested, "Why don't you continue your conversation over lunch?"

"I hope," my landlord said, "that a light lunch will be enough. Now that there's so little food to be had, you'll have to excuse my wife for not making what she did before the war."

As we ate, he told me more about himself. He was a dealer in cooking oils, of which he had been a major supplier. When the war cut into his business and its profits, he decided to liquidate it. Although by then not much was left of it, there being no cooking oil available, he still owned various assets, which he was now selling off one by one.

As soon as the last of them was disposed of, he and his wife planned to retire to a small village in Bavaria where there were no shortages. He would read his books and they would live out their lives there, far from the war and the world that would come after it.

That same day the Lichtensteins moved me to a bigger room and invited me to eat with them regularly; Frau Lichtenstein also offered to take care of my laundry and my other bachelor chores. Yet when the time came to pay my rent, I was billed for the smaller room, with not even a service charge for my additional expenditures.

The rabbis tell us to pay tribute to the hospitality shown us. Now that I've praised my landlord and landlady, I'll say a few words about the guests they had in their home. Every one of them was proof of how foolish our Eastern-European prejudices toward German Jews are. Although there may be other Jews who are more learned, pious, and perfect in their faith, the Jews of Germany yield to none in their honesty, trustworthiness, responsibility, and common sense. Moreover, Herr Lichtenstein's library made me realize that all our knowledge of Jewish history, philosophy, and literature are but the crumbs fallen from the tables of those great polymaths, the scholars of Jewish Germany. There are books we never would have read had we not happened to be in the same place with them. The Lichtensteins' home was the best course I could have taken in the achievements of German Jewish scholarship.

These halcyon days did not last long. A newspaper publisher purchased the Lichtensteins' building and paid the tenants to vacate it. The Lichtensteins had to move—not to where they had planned to, but to where plans had been made for them. Their only daughter, whose husband was killed in the war, had been begging them to come live with her, it being too much for her to earn a living and look after her children at the same time. When the Lichtensteins left their apartment, they moved to hers. Just in case things didn't work out there, they also bought a place in an old age home. I moved the same day they did and was once again without a room.

This was how I met Simon Gabel, who had been hired by the publisher to renovate the building and redo its interior. Simon Gabel was a great architect. He was attuned to the spirit of the times and understood its needs. There wasn't a wasted or an extra inch of space in anything designed by him. Whatever you saw was there because it had to be.

Different generations, different houses. Once, when people's needs were smaller and their hearts were larger, they preferred ornament to convenience; we, whose needs have grown as our hearts have shrunk, like it the other way around. No modern architect, it must be said, equaled Simon Gabel in this respect. If every nouveau-riche family and up-and-coming corporation sought to engage his services, this was because he knew their needs and catered to them.

Although Simon Gabel had heard of me, he had forgotten where. Indeed, his first words when introduced to me were, "Help me to remember who told me about you." I racked my brains and in the end made a joke of it by saying, "If it wasn't some millionaire, I have no idea."

"Bingo!" Simon Gabel exclaimed. "The other day I gave Brigitta Schimmermann a lift to Leipzig. She was going to pay a condolence call on Dr. Mittel, whose son was killed at the front, and she. mentioned you. I just can't remember why."

And so once again I had no roof over my head. When the Lichtensteins moved, I moved with them. A publisher had bought their building and was redesigning it for the times, in which everyone not killed in the war or because of it wanted to read about it. This was the job of the press: to distinguish the living from the dead by reporting on the dead to the living. If you were alive you read the newspapers, through which the lifeblood of the times circulated: birth and marriage notices, anniversaries and obituaries, commodities and stock prices, and the like. Moreover, reading a newspaper spared you the trouble of forming your own opinion, since there was nothing too complicated for a journalist to educate you about in simple language. In no time you crisscrossed the world and the world was yours for the price of a newspaper. And since there were more newspapers than space to produce them in, good, solid apartment buildings were being converted into editorial offices, presses, and warehouses. Thirty-three families had lived in one building, and one publisher was enough to make them leave.

I was back to combing the streets of Berlin in search of "For Rent" signs. Since there were rooms to rent and I was looking for a room, I can't tell you why a room and I had so much trouble getting together. I looked at each one, pacing off the angles between its walls like the arms of a compass and leaving it in vexation for the next room. Either the rooms were not rooms or I was not myself because of the death of Mittel's son. A man has an only son who volunteers for Germany's war, and Germany's war sends a bullet to kill him. Isaac Mittel had paid his debt to Germany and his son had paid for his patriotism.

At one point I ran into someone with whom I had once lived in the same boarding house. We stopped to chat and I told him about my problems.

"You change rooms too often," he said.

I sent regards to his wife when we parted. "If you're referring to that woman you met me with," he said, "she's no longer my wife. I divorced her and married someone else."

Although I could have told him he changed wives too often, the analogy was imperfect, since he had found another wife and I hadn't found another room.

You'll never guess whom I ran into next. If you'd like a hint, it wasn't someone I was thinking of. You may remember Frau Trotzmüller's daughter Hildegard. I was walking down the street one day when there she was with her brother Hanschen. Hildegard said hello, her eyes widening beneath her narrow forehead. I said hello back, thanking God for having made all human beings different, since I would never have recognized her if not for her eyes. At the Trotzmüllers' I had always seen her in a short dress, the kind that was fashionable the year before the war, whereas now she wore a top hat, a dress down to her ankles, and leather gloves up to her elbows.

"It's so nice to see you," Hildegard said. "We often wonder why you never show your face."

Turning to her brother, she said, "You remember this gentleman, don't you? You took the same train to Berlin."

Turning back to me, she said, "Isn't he a darling? We're going to the tailor to make him a new suit."

Turning to her brother again, she said, "And when Hanschen puts on his new suit, he'll be a new person."

We stood and talked. Hildegard spoke to me and to her brother in turn, and I addressed them both. There are words for every occasion. What a pity there aren't occasions for every word.

We had already said good-bye when she remembered something. "We received a food parcel for you. There were all kinds of good things in it. We kept it until they went bad. If it hadn't had your name on it, we would have been sure it was for Isolde Müller. We'll soon be celebrating her engagement to her next-door neighbor, Friederich Wilhelm Schmidt, the Tax Bureau official from the room opposite Hanschen's. Listen to what happened. Once Isolde asked Friederich Wilhelm for some tax advice. He advised her and kept it up until they decided to get married. Lucky them! They're already living in the same boarding house and don't have to look for another. With every mouse hole full of people these days, they'd never find anything. And where are you boarding? I'll bet it's someplace nice. Your kind always does well."

When she was gone, I lit a cigarette and threw away the empty pack. A man came along and asked for directions to the post office. He was a Saxon, to judge by his accent, and he was holding a little girl by the hand.

"Come with me," I said. "I'm going there myself."

Mention of the food parcel had reminded me that I should sit down and write my cousin Malka, and having no other place to do it, I decided to write her from the post office. On our way the man told me he was from Leipzig and worked in a foundry, and that he had come to Berlin to fetch his daughter, who had been staying with his wife's sister, a tavern keeper in Pankau. They had hoped to put some weight on the child, since the swill in Leipzig had reduced her to a mere shadow of herself. You couldn't even get lard, in lieu of which the city council had issued a vegetable substitute that no self-respecting Christian would touch. The Leipzigers called it Hindenburg lard and said it tasted like the grease with which the city's royal monuments were polished. Yet even though the child had been starving in Leipzig and could eat all she wanted in Pankau, where her aunt ran rings around the rationing bureau, she was so homesick that she had gotten even thinner and had to be taken home to her mother. He had come for her yesterday from Leipzig and they would catch a train back tomorrow. Actually, he would have liked to spend another day in Berlin, a city he had never been in before whose sights he wanted to see, but he had a mean boss to reckon with. Not that he had anything against bosses, because who didn't have one? But this one was an ex-fellow worker who had been promoted when the old boss was drafted, a swinish son of a bitch, although it might be better to call him a low-down bitch of a swine. Either way, the swinehound had taken to ordering his old buddies around. Whatever you asked him for, he said no. He hadn't even wanted to give permission for a trip to Berlin, which he had only agreed to—and just for one day!—if it was taken as unpaid vacation. Promote a man and you promoted his worst qualities. And now he saw he would need two days in Berlin. It was just the excuse the swine-hound needed to call him on the carpet and dock his pay. That's why he was going to the post office to send a telegram, so that he couldn't be accused of taking an extra day without permission.

"We're here," I said.

"This isn't a post office," said the little girl.

"Why isn't it?" I asked her.

"Because our post office is a hundred times bigger," she said.

"Don't exaggerate," said her father. "No building in the world is a hundred times bigger than this one."

"Our post office is a hundred million times bigger," the little girl said.

"You're just being stubborn," said her father. "I tell you no building is a hundred times bigger and now you say a hundred million. Do you know how big a hundred million is?"

"Is it as big as the black man who sleeps in Auntie's bed?" the little girl asked.

"That," said her father, "is a very foolish question. Now let me write my telegram."

I said good-bye to him and his daughter and bought a postcard to send to my cousin Malka. While I was picturing that dear woman living all alone, far from her husband and son at the front, I thought of Mittel's son and the day he left for the war. Mittel was sad that he had raised a son to be a soldier, and his wife was glad that her boy was going off to defend the Fatherland.

That same day Mittel told me the following story.

Heshl Shor, the publisher of the Hebrew periodical *He-Halutz*, had an only son who was up for an appointment to a lectureship at the Sorbonne. One day, as Heshl Shor and his wife were having lunch, he looked out the window and saw the postman. "He must be bringing good news," Heshl Shor said. "Our son's appointment has come through." He rose from the table and went to greet the postman, who handed him a telegram with the news that his son had died. "What a pity!" Heshl Shor said, wiping the food from his mouth. "He was a good lad, a good lad!" And though he returned at once to his lunch, he never changed his menu or his clothes again for the rest of his life. Every day he ate the same meal and wore the same shirt and pants.

I sat and wrote Mittel a condolence note. A few days later I received a reply with details of his son's death. In a postscript he wrote:

"I'll tell you in a whisper what a German professor, the pride and joy of German science, said to me when I sent him my condolences for a son killed at the front. 'For this war,' he wrote, 'we can thank a generation of German teachers who instilled in their pupils the absurd belief that they were the heirs of ancient Greece and Rome.'"

Chapter ten

I found a room. Or rather, out of sheer sadism, it found me. That is, it was a perfectly nice, well-furnished room with decent landlords and it even had two windows. Yet beneath one was a butcher shop that smelled of freshly slaughtered meat and beneath the other was a streetcar stop. The streetcars came and went with a racket one after another, rattling the building, and most of all, me. And late at night, when they stopped running, the building was its own source of woe. My landlord managed a movie theater in Hallensee, and he and his wife came home after the last show and stayed up late, eating, drinking, discussing their affairs, and arguing about box office hits. Worse yet, staying up all night made them sleep all day, so that I had to move around as if in shackles to avoid waking them.

I lit a cigarette and stood looking out the window. A long line of housewives formed a queue stretching halfway up the block in front of the butcher shop, whose raw, bloody carcasses of calves, pigs, rabbits, and poultry hung from hooks on the sidewalk. Each housewife held her ration book high to claim her share of the kill in the name of her menfolk fighting for Germany. The butchers were too deep in blood to notice. It glistened more brightly than the blood of the battlefield, which seeped into mud and earth from corpses that sometimes were shattered to pieces and sometimes rotted away, whereas the flayed flesh on the sidewalk still oozed with life. The head butcher stood in his shop like a general commanding his troops. Although the foe was only slaughtered animals, whoever ate them ingested the spirit of warriors.

But let's put the butcher shop aside and return to the other window, the one facing the streetcar stop. The cars come and go in a hurry, as do the people rushing to board them. Although I might as well be in shackles as in fear of waking my landlord and his wife, my mind is free to roam and it wonders: who started this race, the people or the streetcars? Since it's impossible to think with so much noise, I never come to any conclusion.

Meanwhile, the house begins to stir. My landlord and his wife awake. Doors open and shut. I'm freed from my chains and my landlord feels free to drop in on me. "What's new in the paper?" he asks, lighting his pipe.

I tell him that I don't read the newspapers. This causes his eyebrows to shoot up and his stomach to shake with merry esteem, as if he has never heard such a good joke in his life—and the next day, in the hope of hearing an even better one, he repeats the same question. And having been told that I'm something of an author, he asks, "*Was macht die Kunst?*"—meaning, how is Art these days?

Erich Walter Tanzmann, to call my landlord by his name, came from the celebrated Tanzmann family, which boasted well-known actors, radio personalities, critics, and humorists in its ranks. He had a big face, a big body, and a big belly; as for his heart, I'm no cardiologist. Dark-haired when younger, his pink skull was now smooth and shiny, and he was clean-shaven as was the fashion in bohemian circles; yet being a man of character who wasn't too busy to honor his ancestors' God, he shut his movie theater and went to temple on the High Holy Days. That's Herr Tanzmann in a nutshell. I could say much more about him, because he was always in my room.

As he sat there, he puffed on his pipe and told me what he thought about the world and its machinations, and about the countries that had blundered into joining the enemies of the human race by making war on Germany. When the turn of the English came, he shifted his pipe to the corner of his mouth and said: "To think that we envied them! How we looked up to them and wanted to be like them—and now we see how wrong we were, how completely wrong. Why, they're criminals, plain and simple! And what intriguers! All they know how to do is turn one country against another. But we have integrity and justice on our side and we'll triumph, there's no doubt of it. They'll never get away with it. The truth will win out. Our Kaiser and our fighting men are stronger than their king and all his Tommies. Victory will be ours for sure."

He went on in this vein until his wife brought him the newspaper. Although you might think he would have insisted on seeing it first, men being more curious than women to know what is happening in the world, he let her go before him because of the food columns. These informed her what was available in the market that day, so that she could buy it before anyone else did.

Annalise Tanzmann was a good-looking woman of medium height with an amber, almost golden complexion. She had a wide mouth and thin lips, over which hung a sad, rueful look. Perhaps this came from being childless. The first time I saw her, I was sure she was Jewish. The second time, I was sure she wasn't. The third time, I wondered what made me so sure the first two times. In the end, Herr Tanzmann informed me that his wife had a Jewish father and a German mother. Once, German women sought out Jewish men, who were known to make faithful husbands and good fathers who didn't drink. Nowadays, the only difference between a Jew and a German was that some Jews went to temple and most Germans didn't like Jews.

After Frau Tanzmann brought the newspaper, Herr Tanzmann opened and read it, commenting on each item until the smell of coffee percolated to my room. Soon Frau Tanzmann would appear and say, "I hope you don't mind breakfast being a bit late today. Come join us." Since it was already noontime, I skipped breakfast and went out for lunch.

The restaurant in which I ate in those days was a wartime establishment. Its owners were a wealthy Russian Jew and his wife who had been taking the waters at a German spa when the war broke out and trapped them in Germany. Strapped for cash, since the German banks had stopped honoring Russian accounts, they sold their valuables and opened a luncheonette. At first their friends came to eat there, and then their friends brought their friends. As I didn't eat meat or anything cooked with it, I would ask for a scrambled egg and salad, for which I was charged double for a special order. Why then, you may ask, didn't I go to a vegetarian restaurant? If I tell you it was because there were no Jewish ones and I didn't trust Christian cooking, you'll accuse me of being a religious fanatic. Let's just say, then, that I was afraid of being served worms from unwashed vegetables.

Apart from myself, the restaurant's customers were all Russian Jews. Some had come to Germany to study and others for reasons of business or health; all found themselves out in the cold when the war began. The students were dismissed from the universities, the businessmen were put out of business, and the medical cases not only failed to regain their health, they had new complaints added to their old ones. Tossed ashore in a foreign country at war with their own, these fellow sufferers put up with its hostility in silence and dreamed of rejoining their friends and families in Russia and resuming their old lives there. They met regularly in the restaurant to discuss favorite subjects and talk about the day they would go home—for even though they knew they were going nowhere as long as the fighting continued, talking about it was the next best thing. Their longing made Russia seem like a utopia inhabited by the world's most virtuous people, and even those of them who at first had hoped as Jews for a Russian defeat were now praying for a Russian victory.

As enemy aliens, all of them, except for a few with high connections, had to report every day to the police. As an Austrian, on the other hand, I only had to notify the police when I changed addresses. In the Russians' eyes this gave me a special standing with the Germans, let alone with German Jews. I'll give you an example of the ridiculous lengths it went to. One of the restaurant's customers, a young university student with a German mistress, had received a monthly allowance from his wealthy father in Russia before the war. Now, afraid his mistress would leave him because they had no money to live on, he came to me and said: "Look, you can see I'm in a fix. Do me a favor and ask the president of the temple to get my girlfriend a paying job in the High Holiday choir."

Since most of the customers had little to do, they sat around chatting after lunch until it was time to report to the police. Unable to get any rest in my boarding house, I joined them. There was one of them whom I sometimes walked back to his room. Although it wasn't as nice as mine, it didn't smell like a butcher shop or shake from streetcars. Standing at its window while watching the sun set and the first stars appear in the sky, I thought of sitting on my balcony in Jaffa, a tranquil evening sweetening my solitude. Now, there was no way of returning there or escaping the din of Berlin.

One night, kept from sleeping by the noise and the smells and still other things, I made up my mind to move. The next morning I told Frau Tanzmann. "Very well, very well," she said with an insulted look, as though I had something personal against her. Yet the Tanzmanns continued to be friendly. In this they were unlike other landlords, who hounded their tenants from the day they were given notice. In light of the housing situation, my decision began to seem to me impetuous. Yet while I knew from experience how hard it was to find a room, knowing and doing were two different things. And if I've spoken well of some of my landlords, let this be my witness that I'm neither a grouch nor a misanthrope when I criticize others, but am simply assigning praise or blame where it belongs.

After searching everywhere, I rented a room in a nice-looking building on Dahlmannstrasse, off the Kurfürstendamm. As winter was setting in and the room had central heating and was near an underground station, I overlooked its drawbacks. I had despaired of finding the ideal place and only wanted somewhere I could fall asleep in, and when I came across a room for twenty-eight marks with a landlady who looked reasonable, I took it. The rent included a breakfast of three slices of bread with jam and a cup of wild chestnut tea, as well as a cup of real tea every afternoon. In fairness to my landlady, she not only kept her side of the bargain, she also brought tea for my guests. In fairness to myself, I tipped her well for every cup she brought.

My room was long and narrow and suggested an animal's maw—and if there is no such creature, there should be. It had one window, facing north, with a desk and a couch; a round table between them to eat on; and a clothes closet and bed on the desk's other side. I've already told you that I didn't own much clothing, having given away my old things and never bought new ones. Mostly I used the closet for storing the manuscripts I had given up working on, plus a few books from my parents' home in Galicia.

I like looking out windows and I looked out this one, too. It faced a courtyard with a view of thirty-six kitchens, whose clashing smells informed me what was cooking in the pots of each. Were I a writer of cookbooks, I could have sniffed out enough recipes from the sub-smells of these smells to publish a book on them. Not being one, however, I kept the window shut and spent my time ensconced in my bed, as the room was too narrow for pacing. The bed was next to the door, about which I'll eventually have a few words to say. Overhead, in the room above me, lived a soldier who had lost a leg in the war and now had a prosthesis. He and it were still learning to walk together and to figure out what sort of leg it was. If my landlady was right about its being made of rubber, and not of wood as I thought, it was even more remarkable how so soft a material could thump against a floor like that, let alone against a floor that was my ceiling.

There was nothing to do but trust in time, which sooner or later sees to all things. Either, I told myself, the soldier will drop from exhaustion, or else his leg will, or else I and my thoughts will. Meanwhile, time was taking its time and I lay on my bed thinking. One thing I wondered about was whether the soldier wore a rubber or a wooden shoe on his false leg when he went out. It couldn't have been a leather one, because the shoemaker who cut out the imp's tongues had no leather left to make shoes with.

Every morning when I went to the bathroom, the bathtub was full. One day it had dirty linen in it, the next potatoes, the next cauliflower, cabbage, broccoli, and other vegetables, and before Christmas, meat from the countryside. Prior to marrying Herr Munkel, an employee of the municipal train system, my landlady had worked on a country estate near Potsdam, and its elderly owner liberally continued to bestow on her produce you couldn't find in the city. And when the estate owner wasn't looking, his steward added more.

"This isn't what bathtubs were made for," I said to Frau Munkel.

"Nowadays," she answered quite reasonably, "one doesn't stand on ceremony about such things."

I thought of the use I, too, had made of a bathtub and said with a smile, "But I do have to bathe."

"You can use the sink, *mein Herr*," she said. "If you'd like, I'll bring you a pitcher and bowl."

From then on I bathed every day with a pitcher and bowl, and once a week I went to a bathhouse. Although you may think this was a throwback to my childhood days when I went with my grandfather to the bathhouse before the Sabbath to sit in a tub of hot water, let me assure you there wasn't the slightest resemblance. If I ever write a book about my childhood, you'll see why.

My landlady was tall and thin with a small head, stringy, nondescript hair, an ash-gray face, and eyes the color of kerosene. Yet something about her suggested that when younger she had had no small powers of attraction, nor were men indifferent to her charms even now that she was the married mother of a teenage daughter—at least not to judge by the old estate owner, who treated her generously, always asked about Hedwig, and never failed to include an extra gift for her. His steward did the same, as did the old man's son when he visited the estate.

Hedwig was my landlady's seventeen-year-old daughter. The previous year she had dropped out of school to help her mother, who served lunch every day to six or seven office workers. Actually, there was no need for Hedwig to have done this, as the estate owner had put a thousand marks in trust for her when she was born, to which his son had added more and the steward still more, each without the others' knowledge; she could have stayed in school and even studied to be a teacher, a profession that Frau Munkel considered suitable, having thought highly of it ever since befriending the village schoolteacher while pregnant with Hedwig. Hedwig, however, was keen on housework and preferred the hospitality trade.

Where did I know all this from? Certainly not from the angel of conception, who shared none of his secrets with me. Yet the less a boarder wishes to know about his boarding house, the more he finds out. A good part of my information came from Frau Munkel herself and the rest from the concierge, so that I needed only to put two and two together.

I'm no physiognomist or mind reader, especially when the mind is a woman's. Yet when Hedwig brought my tea, or a letter from the post office, and lingered in the doorway looking at me, it was clear to me what was passing through her head. Here I am alone with a man, she was thinking, and where are all those things that happen in books?

Having discussed Hedwig and her mother, I should say more about my room. It was indeed well heated. This was unusual, coal being needed for the war effort. Yet as the room was squeezed between the kitchen and the bathroom, it benefited from the pipes that led to both. I could have left my window permanently open were it not for the smells of bacon and lard and the scullery talk of the cooks.

And now, having described my room, I'll say a few words about the building. It had several wings and was bounded on one side by the Kurfürstendamm, with a separate servants' entrance and an old gatekeeper who sat smoking his pipe and reading his newspaper. When they weren't being servile themselves, Berlin's gatekeepers acted like lords and made servants of others by insisting they use the back entrance. Besides being true to his profession in these respects, my building's gatekeeper was a wounded veteran of the Franco-Prussian War and would have gladly, were it not for his age, taken on the damnable French once again and made mincemeat of them all. Nonetheless, he found other ways of serving his country. This he did by subjecting every visitor to a thorough grilling, which included an identity check and a business résumé. Since most of my visitors came from Russia or Palestine and spoke with a foreign accent, this German patriot naturally assumed they were enemy agents. Once he turned away a friend who had come to see me. Hedwig alerted me and I went to the gate. "I did it for your own safety, *mein Herr*," he said. "It's my job to keep out spies and saboteurs."

Not wanting to argue with him when a coin would be more eloquent, I tipped him half a mark on the first of the month. This made him eager to prove his mettle, and from then on he jumped to his feet each time he saw me in order to read out Germany's latest victories to me from his newspaper. If I didn't tip him for the service, he gave me a look reserved for spies and saboteurs, and if I did, he broke into a war jingle about the buggering Tommies, the frog-eating Frenchies, the lice-ridden Russkies, and himself, the good German, who would personally drown every mother's son of them in their own blood.

All this upset the gatekeeper's wife, who envied the easy money her husband made and gossiped to me about him. The cad, she said, spent every penny on himself and his stomach and let her go hungry—and as for the wounds he boasted of getting in the war of 1870, he would spend the rest of his life rotting in jail if she ever told the police where they really were from. As this was no business of mine, I tipped her half a mark, too.

My landlady was annoyed at both the gatekeeper and his wife—at the former for making her use the servants' entrance when she came home from the market with her shopping bags, and at the latter for taking unfair advantage of a good-hearted man like myself. Clearly she was of the opinion that I was wasting money on them both that could be put to better use by the Fatherland, for one day she came to tell me that two distinguished ladies wanted to see me. My first thought was that Brigitta Schimmermann was in Berlin and had decided to pay me a call—but who then could her companion be? Enough speculations passed through my mind in the next few seconds to fill an ordinary day. I pictured every socialite I knew in the company of Brigitta Schimmermann, and between one imagined visitor and the next it occurred to me that my beard was uncombed and I was in no state to receive anyone. I was still trying to guess when Frau Munkel asked:

"What shall I tell them?"

"Tell them to come in," I said.

I had never in my life seen the two ladies who entered. Although they looked like ordinary Berliners, they had a la-di-da air. I was wondering what marks of distinction Frau Munkel had seen in them and what they were doing in my room when one of them said:

"You must have heard, *mein Herr*, that the residents of the territories we have conquered are such victims of enemy propaganda that they think we Germans started this war. They have no idea how just our cause is. We, the founders of the Society for the Promotion of Germany in the Conquered Territories, have been publishing pamphlets to correct this misapprehension. Although you may think, *mein Herr*, that I'm speaking of counterpropaganda, nothing could be further from the truth. We simply wish, by means of the... the facts presented in our pamphlets to impress on the previously unaware population of these territories, freed by us from the yoke of Czardom, that it has the good fortune to be... that is, that it is privileged... in a word, that is now under the protection of Germany, which has its best interests at heart."

As she spoke, she kept glancing at her companion as if in the hope of having her sentences completed. Yet no sooner did the latter open her mouth than the first lady continued:

"Furthermore, since Germany's conquests grow daily and the territories continue to expand... that is, since more and more people are seeking Germany's protection... in short, the need for our pamphlets has grown, too. They cost money to publish, and we have taken it upon ourselves, my friend and I, to ask for your help in promoting the cause of justice so as to further the justice of our cause."

So spoke this patroness of Germany while her companion did her best to be supportive, sometimes nodding and sometimes speaking in a dyspeptic voice. I gave them whatever I gave them and sent them on their way.

Subsequently, not a day passed without its charitable cause. Old women, young women, tall women, short women, blond women, dark women, mustachioed women, women thin as broomsticks, women with noses long as vaulting poles, women so obese they looked pregnant or so pregnant they looked obese—they came singly and in droves, all crying: *Mein Herr*, your money, if you please! One had a tongue on which butter wouldn't have melted while another was a belching volcano, but it was always the same refrain: *Mein gnädiger Herr*, give, give for Germany! One woman even registered me as a member in good standing of her society. A good German like me, she said, would get my reward in heaven for every donation I gave her.

I could barely make ends meet and any extra expense meant scrimping on other things, quite apart from the wartime inflation that caused money to melt in one's hands—yet here I was, besieged by wartime appeals. Nor could I refuse to give, since this would have put me under the suspicion of being a bad German. I couldn't even plead illness, because the women collecting for the Red Cross would have called an ambulance. One day I came home from lunch to find my landlady and the representative of a patriotic organization hanging a picture of von Hindenburg over my bed in acknowledgment of my generosity. My fellow Jews from Galicia had named their synagogue for von Hindenburg in the hope of vanquishing their rivals, and I, a peaceable man who would have been happy to vanquish my own bad habits, now had to sleep with him above my head.

In my Leipzig days, I had been friends with Herr König. König was a likable, good-natured man with hands of gold. Everything he did had an artist's flair. Even his Hebrew characters, though not in favor with Isaac Mittel, were popular with the printers. Once he made me a drawing of the Wailing Wall with its tiers of stones and a woman in front of it holding her head in her hands. He did this entirely from his imagination, never having been to Palestine—and when it comes to a country in which even everyday reality is unimaginable, the imagination is never enough. Nevertheless, returning that night to my room and finding von Hindenburg staring down at me, I took out König's drawing and sat looking at it. I almost felt as if God himself was in the room and was determined to bring me back to his holy city. Yet the time had not yet come for a man like me, who still had many hardships and ordeals ahead of him.

Chapter eleven

A kind and clement spring was in the air. Although it wasn't yet felt in my room, I knew it was on its way because of the flowers Hedwig put on my table. There's nothing like saying it with flowers. And there was yet another sign of spring: the central heating had been turned off, the world having begun to warm up. If not for the kitchen smells and the scullery talk, I could have opened my window wide, looked up at the sky, and seen spring dropping down to play—here on a patch of ground, there on a tree branch, there on the first blades of grass between the rocks.

Spring days were tiring and made me want to stretch out on my bed. The minute I did, I heard the rubber leg overhead. I will say this for it, though: by now it had learned the art of being a leg and was a step ahead of its partner, marching in front like the Kaiser's troops on parade. One day, as I was listening to it knock against my ceiling, there was a different knock on the door, and before I could say "Come in," the knocker was in my room. But I should tell you that I'm turning back the clock, because all this happened at the beginning of my stay at Frau Munkel's.

You may remember Hanschen's sisters. Although they never paid me any attention when I boarded with them, I rose in their estimation when I left them. The first to let me know this was Hildegard. One day, when I bumped into her in the street, she complained that I never visited her family. Now that I lived on Dahlmannstrasse and she lived on Fasanenstrasse, both of which ran into the Kurfürstendamm, we often met on the streetcar and chatted. Hildegard, as you know, had two sisters—and it was one of them who knocked on my door that day. Although it could have been either Gert or Lotte, I'll state for the record that it was pert little Gert. What had brought her? Gert worked in an orthopedics store that had sent her to deliver a new rubber strap to the soldier above me, and hearing that the ex-boarder in Hanschen's room lived one flight down, she had come to inform me what I already knew from Hildegard, namely, that a parcel had arrived in my name. Her family had kept it until it tore and fell apart, but from now on, Gert said, she would bring me any parcels addressed to me.

Although no more parcels arrived, this didn't stop Gert from returning. My cousin Malka, who knew about the intellect, knew something about the stomach as well. Not only had she given me a goose liver, she had sent a package of food to Berlin for me. Inasmuch as I had passed the liver on to Hanschen and the food in the parcel went bad, I had no pleasure from either. Yet meanwhile Hanschen was restored to his mother and Gert had come to my room to let me know that she would come to my room to let me know if any more parcels arrived.

As she sat there, Gert told me how she had discovered I was boarding with Frau Munkel even though my name was not listed downstairs. It so happened that when the boarder before me was removed from the directory no one else was put in his place, and Gert, who noticed such things, asked Hedwig who the new tenant was. She had a habit of reading directories, Gert told me. Even if they never changed, and the same Miller went on living opposite the same Schmidt with the same Meier between them and the same Cohen and Levi one flight up, she studied each name so carefully that she sometimes forgot the errand she was sent on. Naturally, her employers scolded her—most of all, the store's owner. But although Gert was afraid of being fired for this, it wasn't why the owner was irritable. The real reason was that she was in love with an officer at the front to whom she sent gift packages and feared being jilted by when the war was over and he no longer needed them. Since no German officer would stoop to marry a Jewess, all his love letters could then be used for wrapping paper.

"Gert," I said, "has it occurred to you that you've forgotten your errand again and haven't delivered your rubber strap? It will be your fault if that amputee never walks again."

Gert's barleycorn of a nose jutted up in amazement that I knew all her secrets.

"You'd better hurry," I said.

Gert's nose vanished. Her slit of a mouth opened and out came a muffled plea not to be banished from my room.

And what brought Lotte? Since Lotte worked as a volunteer for the same patriotic organization that had registered me as a member, you might think she saw my name on its list of donors and came to thank me. If you did, you'd be wrong. Actually, I was visiting my good friend Peter Temper in the zoo and had gone to the bird house for a look at the peacocks. What made me do this was having remembered hearing as a boy that peacocks had beautiful wings but ugly feet, so that they went from laughter to tears and back again as they glanced at one or the other. Childhood memories are powerful even if we know they're not true, and I decided to see for myself. I was scrutinizing a peacock, whose eyes were darting this way and that, when the woman beside me tossed her chin and lisped, "The darling, what feathers it has!" One thing led to another, and Lotte and I linked up, saw the rest of the animals together, went to a café for a cup of what was called coffee, and talked about whatever it was that people talked about during the war. Perhaps we also discussed other subjects. When I stand before the Hearer of All Things and am reminded of everything I've said, I'll know what I said then, too. A few days later, as dusk was falling, Lotte came to my room.

I have to confess that Lotte, though plump, wasn't really so round as the initial impression she made on me and that I may have done her an injustice in describing her. She was tall and buxom, and that day she wore an elegant fur coat with a top hat and carried a riding crop, which was the fashion even for women who had never ridden a horse in their lives. The first thing she did upon entering my room was hang her coat on the window frame, blocking our view of the thirty-six kitchens and vice versa. Next she threw her hat on the bed, then moved it to the table, and then went to the mirror to primp her brown hair with a laugh. From there she sat herself down in the chair by my desk, gave her chin a toss, and lisped with a glance at me, "So this is where you live, in this little box."

On Lotte's next visit she leaned back in the same chair and laughed again, this time at how her dress hiked up when she propped her feet on the heating pipes. The time after that, she picked up the inkwell on my desk and asked:

"Where is the pen?"

"I use a fountain pen," I said. "I keep it in my pocket."

She nodded dismissively and said, "I don't think much of pens that write by themselves. They make me think of pencils, and pencils remind me of dry old bachelors." Opening a drawer of the desk, she saw some Hebrew writing, asked if it was Esperanto, and declared without waiting for an answer, "Esperanto and Sanskrit have the same alphabet."

Lotte had itchy fingers. Whatever she saw in my room, she had to touch. If she had found the Kaiser sitting there, she would have reached out and fingered his mustache. And there was something else about her, too, which was that everything she saw or said made her laugh. This made sense when propping her feet on the heating pipes, since she had nicer legs than peacocks. But what was so funny about Isolde Müller marrying Friedrich Wilhelm Schmidt or Friedrich Wilhelm Schmidt marrying Isolde Müller? To be a polite host, I asked:

"Does Hildegard think their marriage is funny, too?"

Lotte laughed and said, "Hildegard has strange ideas for a woman, especially when it comes to marriage."

To remain polite, I asked:

"Where did she get them from?"

"We have an aunt," said Lotte with another laugh, "Aunt Clotilde. If you saw her, you'd swear she was Jewish, even though she's as Catholic as the Pope. That's because she comes from Spain and you can't get more Catholic than that. Hildegard was raised by her. Once our parents had a fight and our father lost his temper and said Hildegard wasn't his child. Aunt Clotilde heard and took Hildegard to live with her until our father was killed. Hildegard's ideas come from her."

Since Lotte had mentioned marriage, religion, and nationality in one breath, I began to discourse on all three. It didn't take long to realize this wasn't the time or place for it. Subjects that were talked about elsewhere were apparently not meant for my room, and so I dropped them and asked:

"Just what does your aunt do besides look Jewish?"

"Why, she's Clotilde Trotzmüller," said Lotte, tossing her chin, "the head of the Tattersaal, the riding school in the Tiergarten. She's one of the most famous equestrians in Berlin. They say that when she was young she rode horses like the Devil rides his horned goat. Even now that she's getting on in years, she can beat any Prussian cavalry officer in a race. At first she was an instructor in the Tattersaal, where all the high-society ladies learn to ride, and now the whole place belongs to her. Do you know how she came by it? It was because of her husband, Uncle Heinz, our father's brother. Not that Heinz ever gave her a penny. Far from it: she even had to pay for their marriage out of her own pocket—for the curate, the guest carriages, the wedding banquet, everything. Uncle Heinz was much too refined to think about money. What he did best was bow and scrape for the ladies who came to the Tattersaal. Well, one day Aunt Clotilde took a few days' vacation in the Thuringian Mountains with a friend. On their way, near Eisenach, they quarreled and Clotilde turned around and went home. She tiptoed into the house and up the stairs to surprise Uncle Heinz, certain he would be thrilled, because they had a great love. She so adored him that she sometimes swept him off his feet and onto a horse and made it gallop while she clapped her hands like a little girl playing with her dolls. But when she tiptoed into her bedroom, there was Heinz in bed with another woman, naked as the day they were born, with their clothes flung all over. Clotilde took the clothes and threw them out the window—they lived on the top floor—and then she locked the clothes closet, curtsied to the woman, said, 'Adieu, my dear baroness, have a pleasant life with your lover,' and walked out. A policeman found the clothes and took them to the police station. They were identified as belonging to the wife of a ranking baron, an intimate of the Kaiser's, it was said, and he was duly informed. But what could the baron do? It was beneath him to challenge a riding teacher to a duel, and divorcing his wife was a bad idea, too, since she was the daughter of a Graf and stood to inherit two large estates, one from her father and one from her mother, apart from their having two lovely children. And so he took the baroness back, got Aunt Clotilde and Uncle Heinz to make up, and bought her a controlling share of the Tattersaal. Later on she bought out the other shareholders, and now the place where she used to teach is hers lock, stock, and barrel. It's from her that Hildegard gets her ideas about marriage, clothing, and everything."

Lotte laughed and lisped, "But what am I telling you about my aunt for?" She wasn't laughing at Clotilde, who disapproved of levity because it led to sin, but at herself, for boring me with stories that sounded taken from a penny novel. Yet since I was clearly a person who could have all the stories in the world fobbed off on him and still be ready for more, she went on telling me one after another about her father, and her mother, and their marriage, and her mother's heartbreak when her father was killed in a duel, and Hanschen's disappearance in the war, which broke her mother's heart even more. Now Hanschen was back with his family, but Frau Trotzmüller was not back to her old self.

The wartime shortages had made it impossible to buy the chocolates and sweets one normally offered to a young female visitor, especially if one had no talent for befriending the salesgirls in the confectionary shops. I wondered what I might serve to Lotte and thought of a cup of tea. Before I could finish ringing for room service, Hedwig was at the door. In case you're marveling at her efficiency, you might as well know that she had been standing with her ear glued to it all along. And with that I've kept my promise to say a few words about the door.

I sat drinking tea with Lotte and eating spoonfuls of huckleberry jam sent to Frau Munkel by the old estate owner or his steward. It was ironic to think that whereas I had always drunk my tea alone when boarding with Lotte's family, now that I boarded with Frau Munkel I was drinking my tea with Lotte. Not that she and I had nothing to talk about. When I stand before the Hearer of All Things, I hope I'm not reminded of everything I said to that Trotzmüller girl.

I might mention at this point that never once did Gert turn up in my room when Lotte was there nor Lotte when Gert was there. Although you may find this strange, it isn't, because if one of them was visiting, Hedwig would tell the other, "He just went out."

"Where to?"

"He didn't say, but I think it must have been to the train station, because I saw him turn right at the corner. If you're quick, you'll catch up with him."

If I was alone when one of the sisters came, Hedwig accompanied her to my room, knocked on the door, and withdrew when it was opened. What *was* strange was that Lotte's hair and fur coat left a scent that lingered, so that Gert should have realized her sister had been there before her. But perhaps this, too, was no mystery, since Gert's nose was too small to smell anything.

When Hedwig saw how sociable I was, she started dropping by too often for comfort—and if told I was busy, she stood shrinking in the doorway with tears in her eyes. This made me feel like giving her as good a scolding as the horseman gives Käthchen of Heilbronn in Kleist's drama, but before I could, either Lotte or Gert would arrive. If it was Gert, I was in for an hour of tedium, and if it was Lotte, she took off her top hat and fur coat, laid her riding crop on my desk, and laughed while fingering whatever she could lay her hands on. The strangest thing, though, was this: when Lotte noticed the drawing of the Wailing Wall above my desk, she neither laughed nor reached out to touch it. She only asked: "Why is that woman crying?"

"She's a mother," I answered. "She's crying for what the enemy destroyed."

I didn't feel like telling her about the Temple in Jerusalem.

"Is that why you're sad?" Lotte asked.

"Sad?" I said. "I'm the happiest man on earth."

"You don't look it," said Lotte.

I said, "Not everyone knows what to look at."

Lotte said, "But—"

"No buts!" I said, interrupting her. "'But' is a word for the mealy-mouthed. Whatever they say, 'but' comes next. A well-brought-up girl who thinks before she speaks never has to say 'but.' I can see you want to say something. I suppose you want to tell me it's a perfectly good word that's found in the dictionary. An objection like that isn't even worth answering, but since I care about you as the sister of the man who carried my bags from the train station to your boarding house, I'll answer it anyway. Did you ever meet anyone who used all the words in the dictionary? And besides, what good are dictionaries with their lists of words that don't belong together and are only there because they start with the same letter? They're like hexameters that have nothing in common but their feet. Look at me, Lotte. Do I ever say 'but' or talk in hexameters? Well, enough of that. Let's hope you never say 'but' again. It's you who looks sad, Lotte. You must think life without its buts wouldn't be worth living. Mind you, I'm not telling you what to do, I'm only giving you some sound advice. Why are you leaving so soon? What's the hurry?"

Lotte had actually had no intention of leaving. It was only my asking that made her go fetch her coat. Not wanting to appear eager to be rid of her, I didn't offer to help her into it. Neither did I compliment her on her hair when she went to the mirror, nor tell her she looked prettier without her hat, since she might have thought I was making up for being rude. It was only when she reached for her riding crop that I felt a need to break the silence and said:

"You call that a whip? I'll tell you a story about a whip that will give you goose pimples. Did you ever hear of a whip that whipped all by itself? No? Then let me tell you about one."

I never did tell Lotte the story of the whip because I was tired of the conversation. But that doesn't mean I can't tell you.

Long ago the Jews of Germany had a custom whereby a man who thought he had sinned would lie down on the doorstep of the synagogue between the afternoon and evening prayers and receive thirty-nine lashes of the whip from the sexton while reciting the Yom Kippur eve prayer that begins, "May the Merciful One atone for wrongdoing." Once, some pranksters with no use for religion or its customs decided to have fun at the sexton's expense and lay down in a group by the door with their faces to the floor and their backsides in the air. The sexton, not realizing he was the butt of a practical joke, was debating how to proceed when a fiery whip with thongs of flame descended from the sky and began to lash out left and right. Had God not had mercy, nothing would have been left of those jokers but their shoelaces.

I walked Lotte to the Trotzmüllers' and said good-bye. On my way back to Frau Munkel's, I ran into a man I knew from the Lichtensteins', though I had met him before that in the Reform temple on the night of the fast of the Ninth of Av on which the war broke out. "Have you heard from Herr Lichtenstein?" I asked him.

"When Balaam," he answered as though asked a different question, "wanted to bring down ruin on the people of Israel, he loosed the Moabite women on them."

You may have heard of the consternation of the great Rabbi Gershom when, confronted by a man who had sinned, he recognized the same evil impulse in himself. And this happened as he was coming from a synagogue, a holy place! Imagine then how someone like me, having just parted from a German woman, felt to be reminded of the Moabites that Israel had whored after—and by a Reform Jew, of all people, the kind we scoffed at for being more German than the Germans.

This marked the end of my relations with Lotte, not to mention Gert, with whom there had been nothing to begin with. Hildegard, I still saw now and then. Sometimes I ran into her in the department store in Westend and sometimes as she was coming home from the rationing bureau with, as she put it, "a sackful of ration books and a thimbleful of food." Once, too, I saw her walking with an old woman who was none other than her Catholic aunt Clotilde, the owner of the Tattersaal. Why Hildegard made a point of stopping to introduce us, I don't rightly know.

Clotilde was wearing a black satin dress with a white lace collar. A light shawl, thrown over her shoulders, was fastened by an ivory clasp, and she had a silver cross on her chest. On her black velvet hat was a brooch made to look like a dove's wing, while a bright copper pin in the shape of a sword was thrust into the hat's hollowed crown. Every finger of her hand, which gripped a green silk umbrella, had a ring on it. Although she may have looked Jewish, there was nothing Jewish about her eyes. They were blue, with long, shiny black lashes and a cruel gleam when they looked at you.

"And who," Clotilde asked Hildegard, "is this distinguished gentleman we have interrupted our walk for?"

"He's the boarder who used to live in Hanschen's room," Hildegard said.

"Does he have anything to do with the Jewish man who brought Hans back in your mother's dream?" Clotilde asked.

"He is that man," said Hildegard.

"Tell me, my dear," Clotilde said to me, "how did you ever make such a dream come true?"

"That," I answered, "isn't something I can tell you while standing on a street corner."

"In that case," Clotilde said, "come visit me. You'll find me in the telephone book. And here is my address."

She took out a striped visiting card and gave it to me. I folded it in two and stuck it in my pocket.

"Where I come from," said Clotilde, "one doesn't treat a visiting card like that."

"I did it purposely," I said. "Now, when I see a folded card, I'll remember who gave it to me."

"Where I come from," Clotilde said, "visiting cards are read before they're put away."

"By waiting to get home before reading it," I said, "I'll only double my pleasure."

Chapter twelve

One day I was waiting for a streetcar. The first one to come along was full. So was the second. Before I could board the third, others squeezed onto it ahead of me. I lit a cigarette and stood watching the traffic. The cars sped by too fast for me to focus on any one of them. Like the thoughts of the passengers waiting for the streetcars, they didn't stand still for a moment.

I tried concentrating on a single thought to pass the time. I don't have to tell you what that's like. One thought leads to another and then to another, and before you know it there are so many of them that you can't remember which came first. I'll try to put them in order, then—if not in the order they occurred in, at least in that of what they were about. And since I have to start somewhere to avoid an infinite regression, I'll begin with wartime Berlin.

I was living in a small, sunless room. I looked for another room and couldn't find one, and so when I received a letter from Dr. Levi's widow asking to consult with me about his books, I set out for Grimma. As I was changing trains in Leipzig, Brigitta Schimmermann saw me and invited me for lunch. Having time on my hands, I went to see Dr. Mittel, only to realize that I didn't know where my lunch with Brigitta was supposed to take place. I journeyed on to Levi's widow, had a frustrating time with her, and accomplished nothing. On my way back from Grimma, I discovered where Brigitta's nursing home was and went to see her. From there I returned to Berlin with a detachment of soldiers, one of them Frau Trotzmüller's long-lost son, who returned with my bags to his mother's. Because of him, I lost my room and had to wander from place to place. After that came still more, some belonging to the category of repetition and some whose purpose was known only to The Solver of All Mysteries. And with that, I believe, I've arranged things better than did my thoughts at the streetcar stop, which jumbled everything while forgetting nothing.

As I've said, it was early spring. The grass was sprouting, the days were growing longer, and the animals in the zoo were fed at five P.M. instead of four. Even the high-society ladies riding their horses in the Tiergarten cracked their whips more hopefully. I alone was still deep in winter. I wore my winter clothes, my room was dark, and I was greeted by thirty-six kitchens and their smells whenever I opened the window. If I lay in bed, the peg leg above me stamped with annoyance. When I went to wash in the morning, the bathtub was full of dirty laundry. Each time I tried to read, I had a visitor, and if I went out, I had to listen upon my return to the gatekeeper's boasts of Germany's victories and his wife's gossip. And once I was back in my room, Hedwig would come to the doorway to inform me that either the big Trotzmüller girl, meaning Lotte, or the little Trotzmüller girl, meaning Gert, had come to see me. Before she was done, Frau Munkel would appear with the news that two patriotic ladies wished to pay a call.

I threw away my cigarette, gave up on the streetcar, and walked. On my way, I made up my mind to move again, this time to a place where nobody knew me or could bother me. If I found something livable, I might even get back to work—if not to actual writing, at least to something like it, such as reviewing my manuscripts and seeing what could be salvaged from them. There was no point in keeping the rest, since whatever isn't destroyed when it should be ends up destroying its possessor.

To avoid revisiting rooms I had already seen, in some cases more than once, I listed all the suitable neighborhoods I still hadn't lived or searched in and in which there was no danger of meeting anyone I knew. Having resided in Charlottenburg, Hallensee, Williamsdorf, and Thuringen, and room hunted in Schmargendorf and elsewhere, I thought it a good idea to try Friedenau.

I had often thought of renting in Friedenau because my friend Peter Temper lived there and sometimes, when I walked him back to his room, we stayed up so late talking that I missed the last train and had to sleep over. The problem was that Peter had nothing for me to sleep on but a tiger skin. It was the room's centerpiece and had to be taken down from the wall above his bed after removing all the bric-a-brac that hung on it.

I went to Friedenau, found an attractive building on a pleasant street with a "Room For Rent" sign, and knocked on the door of the apartment. The woman who opened it had a small face, small teeth, a slim forehead, smooth hair parted in the middle, nervous movements, and a way of talking so quickly that she swallowed the ends of her words. But the room she showed me was nicer than any I had ever lived in, tastefully furnished with a soft carpet and woodcuts on the walls with illustrations from German folktales and the *Nibelunglied*. I plucked up my courage and asked:

"How much is it?"

"Thirty-five marks and five more for breakfast," said the woman.

"If it's available," I said, "I'll move in today."

She licked her lips and said, "It's available. It's been empty since the former tenant left and died a hero's death."

"Who was that?" I asked.

She licked her lips again and said, "My son."

I gave her a down payment and said, "I'll fetch my things."

I returned to Charlottenburg and explained to Frau Munkel why I had to move to Friedenau, surprised by how easily a man like myself could concoct a story. Then I paid the bill, adding a bit extra to keep her from complaining that I was leaving in the middle of the month. She was sorry, Frau Munkel said, to be losing her best boarder.

For all I knew she was telling the truth, even though it must have been a comfort to her that the gatekeeper would no longer be tipped.

Frau Munkel also regretted that, while I was out looking for a room, I had missed the excitement in the apartment opposite my window. The husband of the woman living there had come home without warning from the army and found... but Frau Munkel was ashamed to tell a decent boarder like me what that was. She would tell me anyway, though: it was another man. And where? In the one place no husband wanted to find one. And with whom? That, said Frau Munkel, I could guess for myself. Not that such things didn't happen all the time, but she wished I had been there because this woman was a frightful snob who had looked down her perfect nose at everyone. Now its perfection had been squashed like a ripe pear by her husband, who hadn't spared the rest of her either.

At this point, I should say a kind word about Herr Munkel. If he hadn't helped to transport my belongings on the underground, I would never have found anyone to move me, since all the porters were at the front and those who weren't were impossible to get hold of.

By evening I had moved into my new room in Friedenau. It was large and attractive, with handsome furnishings and lots of air. Since the day I left Palestine, I hadn't lived in anything like it. I sat at the desk and switched on the lamp. The chair was comfortable and everything seemed to welcome me. Even the knight Hagen, looking down at me from the *Niebelunglied*, had a friendly look on his naively cruel face. Leaning back in my chair with a fresh breeze blowing through the window, I thought of other nights, quiet and serene, on which I had once been able to work. I was taking out my manuscripts, which I hadn't touched since the war broke out, when a smell of dog droppings mingled with the breeze. No one had told me that my landlady raised lapdogs. The smell made me put my manuscripts away and pick up a book that was lying in the room, Voltaire's "On The Best of All Possible Worlds." I call it that because of its contents, even though this wasn't the title its author gave it.

In the middle of the night I was awoken by a terrible scream, followed by a volley of curses. This was only the beginning. Night after night I was forced to sit up in bed by screams and quarrels that began with oaths and ended in mayhem. Before long I discovered the reason. My landlord was a violinist who played in a café, and whenever he came home without all his earnings his wife scolded him until they fought and came to blows. More than once I had to leap out of bed and snatch some lethal weapon from one of them. If a night went by without my hearing them, I would fear there had been a double murder.

One night their fight was worse than usual. I jumped up and ran to them. The cause of it this time was their only son, an interior designer who had ordered some expensive furniture for his room. Before he could pay for it he was killed in the war, and when the carpenter came to repossess it, my landlady tried convincing her husband to testify in court that he had witnessed his son settle the debt. Not wanting to go to prison for perjury, he refused.

"What do I care if a dishrag like you rots in jail?" she shouted at him.

"You should care," he shot back. "Who but me would even look at a decrepit old whore like you?"

One word led to another and they were soon at each other's throats. If I hadn't intervened, they would have finished each other off.

But I've gotten ahead of myself. That first night in the room, I sat reading Voltaire on the best of all possible worlds. After a while I grew sleepy, and in my sleep I had a dream. In it I was walking in a valley beneath Baalbek and saw an old crow sitting in a treetop. The crow tossed its head and called, "Arb, arb, arb!" Although it looked like Voltaire, it didn't fool me. It stuck out its beak and said, "Did you hear what I said? I said arb, arb, arb. You thought it was arf, arf, arf, but it's arb, arb, arb. That's why Adam called me *oreb* in Hebrew— *oreb*, mind you, not *orev* as you say today. And by the way, how come we never see you any more at the Jordan, or the Sea of Galilee, or any of the Land of Israel's waters? Do you think you're too pure for the water of the Holy Land?"

When I went to the bathroom in the morning, I found a litter of puppies yelping in the tub. "What kind of place is this to keep dogs in?" I asked the landlady.

"What's wrong with dogs?" she answered. "If you ask me, they're better than most people, let alone that carpenter, who's worse than an Englishman. Just imagine! A woman's son dies fighting for the Fatherland and he comes and puts a lien on her property."

While I wouldn't go so far as to prefer dogs to people, I won't deny that the little rascals sticking out their lickety tongues were cute creatures. Cute or not, though, I had to bathe, and so I agreed to pay my landlady five more marks a month to clear the tub. The pups were promptly moved elsewhere.

At breakfast that morning, I found dog hairs in my coffee. I didn't drink or eat a thing. The next day, and the day after that, and the day after that, I had the same experience. Everything came with dog hairs, the puppies having been moved from the bathroom to the kitchen.

Over lunch with friends that day, I told them of my plight. The jokers made a joke of it, the sympathetic ones sympathized, and the practical ones advised me to move again. As I was thinking about my new landlady and her dogs after leaving the restaurant, I ran into the sculptor Druzi. We chatted about this and that and he invited me to his studio. Although loathe to waste my time, I didn't want to be rude. Before I knew it, we were there.

We climbed the thousand-and-one stairs and reached the loft with its stone and clay figures. Druzi sat me down on a slab of rough stone and said, "Before I show you my work, let's have some coffee." He filled an electric kettle, put it up to boil, and said, seeing the look on my face, "A person might think you'd never seen anyone make his own coffee."

I told him about my landlady and her dogs.

"All the landladies of Berlin be damned!" he said. "I wouldn't drink a drop of their coffee or eat a slice of their bread. And don't think it's because they're stingy. It's because they expect you to live by their timetables. If you want to be free, you'll make your own meals and be independent. Whoever leans on others forgets how to walk."

After parting from him, I went and bought an electric kettle. The next morning I boiled water and drank a cup of tea without dog hairs. For three straight days I made my own tea for breakfast just as

I had done in Palestine, when I was my own master and cooked my meals on an alcohol burner. Not that an electric kettle is as cheery as the flame of a burner, but the tea was the same tea.

On the fourth day, the kettle didn't heat. I went to ask my landlady what had happened to the electricity and ran into her husband. "The bitch is gone for the day," he said. "And if you're wondering about the electricity, she has it in for both of us. She knows my greatest pleasure is reading the morning paper in bed and she shut off the current to make sure I had no light."

We stood commiserating in the dark hallway, one of us without light for his newspaper and the other without heat for his tea, each waiting to be comforted by the other. What he saw in me, I don't know. I'll tell you what I saw in him.

He was a bandy-legged man of average height with a bushy white mustache and large, sad, puzzled-looking eyes. All I remember of his name is that it was French and had a single syllable. He was, he told me, of Huguenot stock, the last of a long line of master violin makers. After he married and had a child, he could no longer afford to make quality instruments and took to turning out cheaper ones of the kind used by country fiddlers and tavern dance bands. His dream had been to go back to his old craftsmanship once his son was self-supporting—and in fact the boy did well in school and earned a degree in interior design. Since a designer needed an office, he and his wife rented a large apartment in Friedenau with an extra room, which their son decorated with a fine carpet and beautiful things in the hope of attracting customers.

Along came the war and the boy was drafted. The longer the war lasted, the harder it became for my landlord to find the right materials for violin making—and in any case, there was no one to buy his instruments, since the younger musicians were all in the army and the older ones already owned violins. He was left without work and couldn't find another job, and meanwhile, prices kept rising and it wasn't a woman's way to economize, especially not a woman like his wife. To take his mind off her, he began to spend his time in taverns, where a man could sit and concentrate on the people around him.

One night he glanced at the tavern owner and saw that the man looked worried. What, he wondered, could be troubling him—had the Spree run out of water? This was his own private joke, since the wartime beer tasted like river water. Yet being looked at makes a person look back and being thought about makes a person self-conscious. The tavern owner grew aware of my landlord's stare and joined him at the bar, and the two began to talk. The owner was worried, it seemed, because his clientele had shrunk. His regular customers were spending less time at the bar, while couples out for an evening's fun had stopped coming because his band had lost its flair after its violinist was drafted. No one wanted to dance to its music any more.

"Perhaps I could fill in for him," my landlord said without thinking.

The tavern owner brought him a violin and he played with the band and was given a night's pay when the tavern closed after midnight. The next night he brought his own instrument and played again and was well received. Besides paying him well, the owner brought him a free pitcher of beer and a plate of blood sausage. Suddenly, he had a way of making a living despite the hard times.

Then came the news of their son's death. As terrible as the death of a child is, it's easier to bear when there are two parents to comfort each other. But not only was his bitch of a wife no comfort, she kept reminding him of his French ancestry, which made him to blame for the death of their son, who had lost his life on the Western front. And now he had a new headache: the carpenter wanted the furniture back and his wife, who had gotten used to it, refused to surrender it. "If you swear in court that you saw our son pay for it," she told him, "there's nothing the carpenter can do." But perjurers could be fined or jailed, and he didn't want to run the risk. "Besides," he said to me, "why shouldn't the carpenter get his furniture back? He wasn't paid for his work or for the wood. He's not a businessman who turns a quick profit; he's a workingman like me who has to sweat for every penny. The carpet is something else. The dealer who sold it to our son on credit is dead now himself, and as long as his heirs don't know about it or want it back, it can stay with us. What does a carpet care if it's on the floor of a room or rolled up in a store or a warehouse? The heirs won't lose their fortune if they have one carpet less. You can't compare it to something made by a craftsman. If you can't pay him, at least give him back what he made. You, *mein Herr*, must agree with me, because I see you're a craftsman too, just like me and the carpenter. We work with wood and you work with a pen. If your tools are lighter than ours, that doesn't make you any less skilled, because it's the product that counts, not the tools."

So much for my landlord. Now let's get back to his tenant. We stood together in the corridor, one of us with no luck with women and one with no luck with rooms; one whose ancestors were exiled from France and one whose ancestors were exiled from the Land of Israel; one a loyal son of the country that took them in and one longing to return to the country they came from. But although I invited him to my room and repeated my invitation when he declined, we went our separate ways in the end, one to feed his dogs and one to eat in a restaurant.

One day I went to visit my friend Peter Temper. It was a Monday, the day on which the big cats skipped breakfast, and Peter had the morning off. As usual, we talked about animals, big and small. After a while we got around to the lions from the German colonies in Africa, and to Hanging Pieters, the pride of the pack, whose condition had worsened and was now incurable. I didn't try to comfort Peter Temper. Instead, I told him about my friend Arzaf in Jerusalem, who got along with every animal and could make them all obey him except for dogs, which he kept away from. Dogs, he said, had nothing they could call their own. They were the mere flux of their human masters, whom they were chained to and sought only to please.

From the subject of dogs I proceeded to the subject of my landlady, who raised them for sale. We talked until it was time for Peter Temper to go to the zoo. He entered by the elephants' gate and I wandered off aimlessly until I found myself near the Russian restaurant, in which I hadn't eaten for nearly a year. Since it was lunchtime and I was hungry, I decided to go in for a meal.

Nothing much had changed. Except for the dishes, which were more chipped, and the waiters' uniforms, which were more frayed, everything was the same. I ate my food and sat chatting for a while with the other customers. When it was time for the Russians to report to the police, I walked one of them to the station house.

Chapter thirteen

The Russian I accompanied suffered from vertigo. In his room, he was sometimes dizzy and sometimes not; as soon as he left it, however, he lost his balance and was in danger of falling. His greatest fear was that this might happen while in line at the police station, where the thought of disgracing himself in front of everyone caused him much physical and mental anguish. My own worry was that, as an Austrian thought to be in the Germans' good graces, I would be asked to intercede and have him released from his obligation. One such imposition led to another. In the end, the Russians always felt I hadn't done enough and the Germans thought they had done more than they had to and made sure to stick me with the bill.

Yet this particular Russian made no demands on me. On the contrary, he did his best to pretend that nothing was wrong. Only after leaving him did it occur to me that I might try to arrange for an exception to be made in his case. I made a mental list of all the people I knew and thought of Professor Nadelsticher, whose recent patriotic book had made a great impression. Even outside of academic circles, it was praised as a scholarly contribution to the war effort.

I knew Nadelsticher from the days when he was working on his magnum opus, *Priests and Priesthood In Ancient Israel.* This isn't the place for an account of the historical debate it set off or an enumeration of those converted to its views. Although I never read it, its thesis, I knew, was that the priesthood was founded by the prophet Ezekiel. Before Ezekiel's time, according to Nadelsticher, ancient Israel had had no priestly class. Like most Christian Bible scholars, Nadelsticher could barely parse a Hebrew verse, let alone read a rabbinical commentary on it; if I was a welcome guest in his home, this was because I had rescued him from more than one embarrassing error of the kind his colleagues were prone to. To his credit, he never sought to conceal the help I gave him. His entire household, down to the maid, always greeted me warmly because they knew he liked me. Once, when asked by a colleague of Nadelsticher's why I never dropped in on him, I answered, "Because your maid isn't happy to see me." "Am I to blame for my maid?" he asked. "When a man is pleased by a guest's arrival," I told him, "so is his wife—and when his wife is, so is the maid."

To get back to my story, I paid a call on Nadelsticher and found him bent over his desk, a manuscript in front of him. The desk was littered with notes, notebooks, articles, page proofs, offprints, and whatever else you might expect to find on a scholar's work table, plus all the Bibles, concordances, and biblical encyclopedias that went with being a Christian theologian. There was also a large, round container that resembled a domed wagon wheel, or perhaps a lady's hatbox—if only, that is, there still were ladies who wore such big hats.

As usual, Nadelsticher greeted me with delight. He had been studying a slate on which he chalked his memos, and his hand, limp and moist when it reached out to shake mine, was not its usual firm self. Realizing it was no time to ask for a favor, I asked if I might smoke. "Unfortunately," Nadeltsticher said, "not being a smoker, I can't offer you a cigarette. But since you are one yourself, it would seem reasonable to assume you've come supplied. Where was I? Ah, yes. The Evangelical Society in Leipzig has arranged a series of benefit lectures for war invalids and I've been invited to give one of them. The society was pleased to hear that I was prepared to speak on the biblical commandment of war, and having reviewed my notes on the subject, I can assure you that its pleasure was justified. And yet—how shall I put it?—my own pleasure is mixed with distress. Perhaps that's putting it too strongly. If one were to objectify the emotion in question, 'a tinge of concern' might be better. The lecture is three days away, and while that's three-sevenths of the time it took Joshua to bring down the walls of Jericho and change the course of history, in my own case it's hardly enough." Nadelsticher pointed with a beefy hand at the hatbox and said, "I can't take that with me" (he gave some reason I don't remember) "but neither can I send it by mail, because I don't trust the post office to deliver it on time."

As this remark may seem a bit obscure, I'll try to explain it. Nadelsticher was a hefty, imposing man who liked to top himself off with a huge, broad-brimmed hat. And yet his everyday hat was modest compared to the even larger one that he wore to his public appearances. He never traveled without it and had to have it with him in Leipzig, to which he couldn't bring it for the reason that I've forgotten.

This hat was a rococo creation, in part like a Rembrandt cavalier's, in part like the cartoon highwayman Rinaldo Rinaldini's, and in part Nadelsticher's version of the hats in the old portraits of the burghers of the Hanseatic League. No one manufactured such things any more, and Nadelsticher had gone to great trouble to find an old hatter, one of the last of his breed, who agreed to make it for him.

"If the police didn't require someone like me to get a permit to go everywhere," I said, telling Nadelsticher of my woes, "I'd bring your hat to Leipzig myself. And yet," I went on, describing my acquaintance who suffered from vertigo, "what I have to go through is nothing compared to the Russian Jews stranded in Germany."

"If your problem is the police," Nadelsticher said, "I can take care of it for you. And as for your Russian friend, give me his name and I'll see to that, too."

Before I knew it he had picked up a telephone and dialed one of the heads of police. By the time we parted, the Russian had his exemption and I had Nadelsticher's hat to bring to Leipzig.

And so once again I was in Leipzig, as at the beginning of this book. Then, however, when I went for Dr. Levi's library, I only changed trains there, whereas now it was a destination in its own right. After depositing Nadelsticher's hat in trustworthy hands, I went to look for Brigitta Schimmermann in The Lion's Den. Not finding her, I telephoned her nursing home in Lunenfeld, got no answer, and decided to pay a call on Dr. Mittel.

Frau Mittel opened the door for me. She was dressed in black and her lips were pursed in stubborn anger. Without asking what I was doing in Leipzig, or uttering more than a few words, she said:

"If you're looking for my husband, he's in his room."

She led me down a long hallway lined with closets and bookshelves. On a shelf was a stack of offprints covered by a drape with cartoons of contemporary scientists and literati, the kind of men Mittel called "the subluminaries of our times." The hallway looped around and brought us to a room with blue walls, a white ceiling, and a piano covered with a green cloth. On the wall above the piano was a photograph of a boy having his cheek patted by Artur Nikisch. The boy, who had just auditioned for the famous conductor, was the Mittels' son. Ignoring the photograph, Frau Mittel knocked on a wallpapered door and told me, "Go on in. You don't have to wait for him to invite you. He doesn't always bother to, but he doesn't mind visitors."

Mittel was wrapped in a house robe, a pile of books in front of him. Other piles lay all around. When I entered, he was occupied with a folder on which was written in Hebrew, *For these things I weep; mine eye, mine eye runneth down with water.* Perhaps it contained letters from his son. Despite having aged greatly since our last meeting, he hadn't lost his sharp edge. Placing a hand on my shoulder, he began to talk as if continuing, even more emphatically, an interrupted conversation. This time, though, he didn't talk about books or the war. Mostly he dwelled on Dr. Levi's widow, who was at death's door but lacked the strength to cross it. If she deserved to be pitied, it was less because she was dying than because she was still alive. Death was the way of the world; what was to be gained by adding useless years to one's life? "Still," Mittel went on, "I'll regret her passing. As long as she lives, Levi's books will be safe. Once she dies, I'm afraid they'll fall into the wrong hands and suffer the fate of all the other books that have been interpreted in ways their authors never meant them to be and would have been outraged by. I wouldn't mind it so much if the misinterpreters didn't then hound whoever disagreed with them. But freedom of thought leads to tolerance; tolerance leads to democracy; and democracy is intolerant. Which, too, might not be so terrible if men weren't gagged in its name—and even then I wouldn't complain if only the gaggers weren't so sure they were on the side of the angels. Well, I suppose they're angelic in their own eyes, because the world has forgotten that there is such a thing as truth, and falsehood has taken its place. I don't know if you've noticed how faces have changed. No one looks cynical anymore. Every face is as open as a movie star's smile. We live in an age of innocence—and precisely that is its cynicism: idealism coupled with evil deeds. You know, I know both my Yiddish and my Hasidism. Now, though, I'm stumped, because I have to testify in court about the Yiddish expression *a khasidisher shmus*. Of course, the judge first summoned some Protestant theologians from the university, but when they couldn't find the words in Gesenius' biblical lexicon, he turned to me.

"What is it all about? It started with a quarrel in the Von Hindenburg Synagogue. One Friday night a Hasid was leading the prayers and taking his time with *Lekha Dodi*, singing and dancing as he prayed. Another Hasid began to grumble. The first Hasid heard him and said with a leer, 'He's in a hurry to get home because he's promised a German officer to let him sleep with his daughter.' Asked how he could say such a thing, he swore it was true.

"The second Hasid went and filed a libel suit. The first Hasid was called to the witness stand. 'What's all the fuss about?' he asked the judge. '*A khasidisher shmus hayst bay aykh a shvuas sheker?*' And now go explain to a court what a Hasidic schmooze is and why an oath taken in the middle of one is no oath. What bothers me isn't that a Hasid bears false witness or that his friend takes him to court. That's human nature. The aggravating thing is—"

Before Mittel could finish his sentence, his wife entered the room with a glass of tea for me, along with some grains of saccharin and a tiny cookie the size of a sugar cube. "You've met my friend before, haven't you?" Mittel asked her.

She nodded, said, "I've met him," and left the room. A moment later she returned and said, "Don't think I bear you any ill will. I simply didn't want to interrupt your conversation. And yet that's just what I've done and meanwhile your tea is getting cold."

While Frau Mittel stood there, her husband regarded her sorrowfully. When she was gone, he seemed about to make some comment about her and then changed his mind. He watched me stir saccharin into my tea and said:

"There's your answer to whoever says that scientists live in an ivory tower. It's just the opposite. Once upon a time the doctors told us that saccharin was bad for our health. Now that there's no sugar in Germany, they tell us how healthy it is. But what were we talking about? About false oaths and tattletales. According to you Zionists, it's our exile that's to blame for our behavior, and all our faults will disappear in a Jewish state. But what if you're like me and don't believe that?"

I stole a glance at my watch without meaning to. Mittel noticed and said:

"When I was young, I didn't own a watch. Now that I'm old and running out of time, I own many. For my sixtieth birthday my wife gave me a Swiss one. But let's get back to our subject. You Zionists are sure that in a Jewish state the Jews will reform. If that watch of yours isn't telling you that you have to go, stay a while and listen to a story.

"Once there was a saintly Jew who committed a minor sin. As you know, from each of our good deeds an angel is born, and from each of our bad ones a devil. The only way this Jew could think of eluding his newborn devil was by moving to the Land of Israel, where devils aren't allowed. Alas, he didn't know that this applies only to pre-existent devils, not to those born from men's sins, who follow them everywhere. In short, he sold his possessions and sailed to Palestine. As soon as he set foot there, he was greeted by a corpulent, distinguished-looking man dressed from head to toe in satins and silks, with a broad sash around his big belly, breeches so baggy you could stick a fatted calf in them, and a long pipe in his mouth, the kind from which the old Hasidic masters used to send columns of smoke to the Upper Worlds while perambulating there themselves. 'Well, well!' he declared to the newcomer. 'We've finally arrived!'

"The saintly Jew was taken aback by the honor of being included in so distinguished a figure's entourage. 'And who, sir, might you be?' he murmured.

"'What, don't you recognize me?' the man said. 'I was born from your sin.'

"'But you were a devil!' exclaimed the saintly Jew.

"'Here in the Land of Israel,' said the man, 'we devils have the good fortune to be allowed to go about as human beings.'

"'And you were thin as a rod,' the Jew said. 'How come you've put on so much weight?'

"The devil smiled and answered:

"'The holiness of the Land of Israel is fattening.'"

Mittel continued:

"When news came of my son's death, a group of Leipzig's leading citizens paid a condolence call. One of them was Luthar von Nietzschke, the great German economist. Unrelated to me, the conversation came around to Zionism. Von Nietzshke said:

"'It makes no sense. Palestine is a small country, without agriculture, without raw materials, with nothing to support a population. How are you Zionists going to settle so many people there? What will they live from? Why, they'll all die of hunger!'

"You know, my friend, that I'm no Zionist and have done nothing to be accused of being one. Nor is there any danger of my becoming one in the years that are left me. Had von Nietzshke and I been alone, I would have corrected him on that score while admitting that Palestine couldn't possibly hope to absorb large numbers of Jews. Our rabbis conceded as much when they stated that, in the days of the Messiah, the Holy Land's soil will give miraculous yields. What better acknowledgment could you ask for that Jews can't live there without miracles? But when von Nietzschke put his question to me, we were in a room with the heads of the Leipzig Jewish community, wealthy Jews who are in love with everything German and hate Zionism like the plague. I sat there thinking: Jewish suffering means nothing to these men and they'll certainly never have to suffer in Palestine—at least, then, let them suffer a bit on my account. And so I said to von Nietzschke:

"'Switzerland is a small country, too. It has no agriculture or natural resources to speak of, but it supports its population very well.'

"'Yes,' he said. 'But Switzerland is known for its craftsmanship and precision industry. There's a great demand for Swiss products. It's a self-sufficient country.'

"I said to him:

"'Surely, *mein Herr,* you know the books of the Prophets and believe in them and in their prophecies of what is in store for us Jews in time to come, such as, *And I will restore thy judges as at the first, and thy counselors as at the beginning: afterward thou shalt be called the city of righteousness, the faithful city.* In the future, then, it's quite conceivable that every international dispute or intractable bit of litigation will be taken to a Jewish court in a Jewish state, where God will appoint worthy judges whose verdicts will always be fair. I'll give you an example from the generation before ours in Germany. There was a great rabbi in Altona to whom Christian litigants used to turn because they knew he handed down prompt and fair decisions, which was more than could be said for the German courts. And it's not just at justice that Jews will excel. They will be renewed in all things and cleansed of the faults that adhered to them in their exile from the wickedness of the Gentiles, as in the words of Isaiah, *And I will turn my hand upon thee and purely purge away thy dross.* There are many other verses that tell of the spiritual rejuvenation and purification of the Jewish people in time to come. And so it's perfectly conceivable that anyone wishing to invest his money safely will ask the Jews of Palestine to manage it, thus fulfilling the vision of the prophet Joel, *And it shall come to pass on that day that the mountains shall drop down new wine and the hills shall flow with milk,* et cetera, et cetera.

"That's what I told von Nietzschke. But what will we tell ourselves? You haven't told me what you're doing in Leipzig. If you've come to buy books, I won't compete with you. I've stopped buying them, and all I do now is rebind the ones that need binding. I don't know who will inherit them or into whose hands they'll pass, but as long as I'm alive I'll take care of the books that took such good care of me. Soon the binder will come to take this pile that I've prepared for him. And you, you're still buying. If the war ever ends and it's safe to travel again, perhaps you'll return to Palestine and take your books with you. I wouldn't advise you to do that, though. Jews and books are better off scattered throughout the world. That much was already known to Jacob in the Bible when he divided his following with all its cattle and camels into two camps, so that *if Esau come to the one company and smite it, then the other company which is left shall escape.* Are you surprised that I still remember my Bible? Since my son was killed, it's the only book I can read."

The maid entered and said:

"The binder is here."

"One mustn't keep a craftsman from his craft," Mittel said. "Let me give him these books and we'll talk some more."

"I'm afraid I have to go," I told him.

"How can I let you go without walking you?" he said. "To tell you the truth, though, I wouldn't have walked you anyway. I can't face going out. All you see are the results of the war: the bloated and the starving and the cripples. By the time the prophet's words, *And they shall study war no more,* are fulfilled, there'll be no one left alive to fulfill them."

I had taken my leave of him when he called me back and said:

"I wasn't telling you the truth. I said I've stopped buying new books, but I do still acquire the occasional missing volume from a set as long as it's not one I really care about. When I arrive at the gates of heaven, I don't want the gatekeepers to think that I've already had all my wishes granted."

Chapter fourteen

After parting from Mittel I walked back to Eisenbahnstrasse, took a room in a hotel near the train station, and again dialed Brigitta Schimmermann's nursing home in Lunenfeld. Once more, there was no answer. Although it wasn't so much Brigitta I wished to see as it was my cousin Malka, I didn't want to impose on my cousin by making her feed me and put me up. And so I stayed in Leipzig, and having time on my hands I decided to visit Herr König, who had given me the drawing of the Wailing Wall. Not knowing his address, I went to the foundry of Kaiser & Partners that cast his Hebrew print.

I arrived at its central courtyard and asked for the main office. A gatekeeper summoned an attendant who took me there. As soon as the manager saw me, he had a chair brought for me. He was comfortably seated himself, surrounded by half-a-dozen men in work-begrimed blue uniforms like a master by his slaves. They were treated brusquely by him, especially one of them, for whom he had harsh words and a glare. When he dismissed them, he said to me:

"You don't recognize me, but I recognized you. Do you remember the man with the little girl in Berlin who asked you the way to the post office and followed you there? That was me."

"How is your daughter?" I asked him. "And how are you? Are you still being picked on by your new boss?"

He bent over, slapped both knees, and let out a long laugh. When he was done laughing, he said:

"You just saw him! That was his head I chopped off and let roll on the floor."

"But what happened?" I asked.

"What happened? It couldn't be simpler. I was given his job, that's what happened. Kaiser & Partners saw that orders were down and decided to reorganize. They sent him back to the factory floor and put me in his place, first of all, because I know the ropes, and second, because I'm good at running things. That's why the Konowitz Evangelical Society elected me to its executive council. There isn't a day when I don't make him pay for treating me like dirt."

I congratulated him and explained what I had come for, and he gave me König's address.

König lived on Kielstrasse, not far from the Brody Synagogue. As I was passing the synagogue, it was time for the afternoon prayer. Since it was that time of day and I was where I was, I stepped in to pray instead of continuing to König's.

Eight or nine men were visible in the dim light. They were standing by their lecterns like intruders in an empty country home, whose owners—the wealthy Jews who paid for the upkeep and sat in the front rows—came only on weekends. The elderly beadle, a short, dignified man with a square, cropped white beard and a high, square yarmulke of the kind popular in Brody when it was still a great market town, walked down the aisle lighting a few candles. He looked surprised to see me: a person my age in the synagogue on a weekday was an uncommon sight. I stayed for the evening prayer too, bought myself some cake in a bakery, and took it back to the hotel for my dinner.

The hotel wasn't fancy and my room was small and not one of the best, since I hadn't wanted to spend money on a larger one. Although I had chosen it for its name, The Temper Hotel, its owner, as I learned from chatting with him, was not a relation of my friend

Peter Temper's. Peter came from an established family and was a descendant of a scrivener in the kitchens of the royal house of Reuss, whereas this hotel was named for the manager of a puppet theater who had opened a small inn for itinerant actors in his old age. When the Leipzig train station was built nearby, one of the inn's waiters bought it from its founder's heirs and turned it into a real hotel. In the end, he went bankrupt and the hotel was sold to settle his debts. Subsequently, it was bought and sold several more times until leased by its present proprietor.

In bed that night, I realized I had run out of cigarettes. I went out to buy some, saw that the shops were closed, and found a café on a side street. It was so crowded that there was no one to wait on me. While I stood there, I noticed a spoon dangling on a chain from the ceiling. Someone saw me staring at it and said, "What are you looking at, man? Haven't you seen a spoon before?"

"I've seen spoons," I said, "I've just never seen one hanging from a ceiling."

"That's because customers ask for spoons to stir their sugar and don't return them," I was told. "This is one spoon they can't steal."

I left the café and turned into Gerberstrasse. Soon I came to a building that, like many of the old houses near the train station, had never been renovated because it was slated to be torn down, and had never been torn down because its owners wished to squeeze the last drop of profit from it. It stood there as it must have in the eighteenth century when Leipzig was a town of twenty thousand people, except that then it had graced the street and now, half a ruin, it defaced it. A slum dwelling in which generations were born, lived, and died, it had one apartment that belonged to a better class of family, the Bieders from Galicia. In my Leipzig years I was a regular guest in Yudl Bieder's home and once attended a Passover seder there. I still remembered the melodies I heard and the dishes made by Yudl's wife Pesl Gitshe. Most of all, I remembered the dances that the two of them improvised with each of their nine daughters after reading the Haggadah. If you ever saw the long cigarettes I smoked before the war, with their brown holders and golden, fragrant tobacco, they were a brand I picked up from Yudl. That's why I was so pleased when, having gone out to buy cigarettes, I found myself in front of his building.

Although Yudl Bieder was in his sixties, he was hale and hearty, and his eyes, which always had a twinkle, shone with love for his fellow man. He was a follower of all the Hasidic rabbis in Galicia, every one of whom stayed in his home when visiting Leipzig, and while a peace-loving man, he prayed in the fractious Von Hindenburg Synagogue. On one day of the year alone, the anniversary of the death of Blume Hasid, the daughter of Reb Yudl Hasid of Brody, whose descendant Yudl Bieder was, did he pray in the Brody Synagogue.

A small kerosene lamp, set inside a sooty lantern, was the only light in the courtyard, in which I had to grope like a blind man's cane. I made my way past barrels, crates, chests, and boards left overnight by the vendors in the nearby market, and finally reached the stairway that led to the Bieders' apartment. Since I knew that the doorbell didn't work and that it would be too noisy inside to hear my knock, I pushed open the door and entered on my own.

A dark little girl with clever, pretty eyes came up to me and asked, "Who are you looking for, mister?"

"For your grandfather, darling," I told her.

She laughed and called out, "Mama, did you hear that? This man also thinks I'm Papa's granddaughter."

This brought Pesl Gitshe, a woman in her fifties dressed like a well-to-do Galician Jewish hostess. Seeing me, she exclaimed:

"There's a true friend, one who doesn't forget those who love him! And we haven't forgotten you either, dear friend! When did you get to Leipzig? Where are you staying? This war just goes on and on. If it doesn't stop soon, the world will be nothing but ashes, God forbid. We have four son-in-laws at the front and four empty beds at home. And our youngest daughters aren't getting any younger and there's no husband to be found for them. It's like a wild beast, this war—it's devoured the best of our young men. I tell you, it's the end of the world! What's the point of sending so many youngsters to be slaughtered? And where are the righteous and their prayers? They've abandoned the world and are silent."

"Let's forget about the war and talk about happier things," I said. "How are you? How is Reb Yudl? And how are Blume, and Rivtshi, and Esther, and Sheyndele, and Iettele, and Tamar? And how is Basha, and how is Reyzele, and what is Amanda up to these days?"

Pesl Gitshe looked amazed. "I swear," she said, "you're the only one of our friends who remembers the names of all our daughters, may each have a long life. You even listed them in the right order."

"How could I not remember them?" I asked. "The Bieder girls are too beautiful to forget."

She couldn't get over it. I didn't tell her that I had made a mnemonic from the first two words of the Bible, *breshit bara*, and that I couldn't have told one of her daughter from another if all nine were standing in front of me, because they all looked alike.

Pesl Gitshe marveled at my memory once more, reached for the little girl's hand, and said to me, "This is our last and youngest. Her name is Tsharny, and *czarny* is the word for her, because she's as black as a stovepipe. But I must say, God be praised, that she's a great joy to me, since otherwise I'd be all alone. All my other girls have grown up and each is busy with something, one at the community center, one at night school, another with music or drawing lessons, another with charity work. You can imagine what it would be like for an old lady like me to have to sit at home doing nothing. Tsharny, my angel, go tell Papa we have another guest. Don't tell him his name. Just say he's a nice man."

"But what's your name?" Tsharny asked. "You can tell me. I won't tell Papa."

"Do you want me to tell you secrets behind your father's back?" I asked.

She threw her arms around her mother's neck, put her mouth to her mother's ear, and whispered:

"Mama, tell me! What's this man's name?"

"Don't say 'this man,'" Pesl Gitshe corrected her. "Say, 'this gentleman.'"

"What's this gentleman's name?" Tsharny asked.

"How can I tell you if he doesn't want you to know?" said Pesl Gitshe.

"You don't know yourself," Tsharny said. "And he doesn't, either. You don't know anything."

As we were talking, Yudl entered the room and said coolly, spying a stranger, "What can I do for you at such an hour, *mein Herr*?" A second later he recognized me, gave me a big hello, clapped his hands, and exclaimed:

"Why, it's providential that you're here! We just mentioned you a minute ago. If this isn't unbelievable, I don't know what is. Come and meet two old friends who would do handstands if they knew you were here. Tsharny, how come you're still up? Go to bed, my angel."

"Papa," Tsharny said, "this gentleman said he came to see my grandfather."

Yudl patted her head and said:

"This was my wife's sixtieth birthday present to me. I told her, 'If you were ready for the aggravation of another pregnancy after giving me nine daughters, couldn't you at least have made it a son this time?' But a woman is a woman and another daughter is what she had. Say what you will, though, this little one is smart as a whip. And you can see for yourself that she's the prettiest child under God's heaven. And now, you little blackamoor, you tipsy topsy flopsy gypsy, you, say good night to me and tell your mama, 'Mama, put me to bed and listen to me say my prayers.' Do that and I promise you'll have dreams like the saints' in heaven."

"Papa," said Tsharny, "that's what you tell me every night, and I still haven't had one dream."

"You're a sillyhead," Yudl said. "You have dreams every night and forget them."

Tsharny asked:

"Papa, what is forgetting?"

"Forgetting," Yudl said, "is what I've done by horsing around with a little pony like you when there are important guests in the next room. Pesl Gitshe, take her and stuff her up the chimney and send us another round of drinks and some of those pepper-and-onion pletzels you baked for the Sabbath, if there are any left."

Yudl ushered me into his room. Before opening the door he said in low tones, "There's someone inside whom you don't know, a good Jew. He's no more of a scholar than are most observant German Jews, who have more piety in them than learning. But his yes is a yes and his no is a no, and you can build a ten-story building on his word."

I followed Yudl and found three men sitting inside: Nachum Berish, Alter Lipa Elbert the slaughterer, and Herr Kitzingen, the Jew Yudl had told me about. Nachum Berish was the rabbi of the Von Hindenburg Synagogue. As I've had occasion to mention, I had helped him to arrange divorces for the wives of Jewish prisoners of war from Russia who had taken up with German women. Although Nachum Berish thought well of me because I refused payment, this also made him suspicious. He was sitting at the head of the table, with Alter Lipa Elbert on his right. Alter Lipa was so devout a Jew that he always introduced himself as Kelbert to avoid having to utter God's name of *El*. Herr Kitzingen sat across from him.

Nachum Berish was short and stout. He had a round, sallow face and two purplish, button-like birthmarks on either side of his nose. Like Alter Lipa, he wore a long coat and a large black hat, the difference being that his coat was made of satin while Alter Lipa's was of a nondescript fabric that had a greenish patina. Each also had a red handkerchief in his shirt pocket, Alter Lipa's for wiping his knife, and Nachum Berish's for business contracts, which were sealed by passing it from seller to purchaser. Although Alter Lipa's dark, bulging eyes didn't suggest a sense of humor, it took little to make him laugh or to infect others with his laughter. A long, bushy beard hung down to his chest and two thick earlocks ran the length of his cheeks. I can't recall whether he was the only Hasid in Leipzig to let his earlocks dangle like that, but most Hasidim tucked them behind their ears.

As for Kitzingen, there wasn't much to say about him. He was neatly dressed with a trim beard, and he seemed to think that mixing a bit of Hebrew with his German and adding a few garbled words meant that he was speaking Yiddish. On the long table was a bottle of brandy, several glasses, and a plate of pastries, beside which the globe of a gas lamp cast an odorous, lively yellow light. While Nachum Berish rose from his seat and held out cool fingertips, searching for a rabbinic bon mot to greet me with, Alter Lipa poured himself another glass of brandy. He raised it halfway to his lips, stopped, saluted me with a toast, downed the brandy, slapped Kitzingen on the back, and said to him, "Do you know who this man is? He's the same person who just made us say, ay ay ay, if only he were here! Now you see how great a Hasid's powers are. And don't think we had to mention his name to make him magically appear. A Hasid can stop the world in its tracks just by thinking. He only uses his vocal chords out of respect for the laws of nature."

Kitzingen shook my hand while glancing at Yudl Bieder to make sure Alter Lipa was telling the truth about me.

We drank another toast and lit cigarettes. Nachum Berish let out a heartfelt sigh and said:

"If you're not surprised to find us sitting together, I'll tell you something that will surprise you."

"Why be surprised to find Jews sitting together?" interrupted Alter Lipa. "On the contrary! A thousand times on the contrary! If anything is surprising, it's that all the Jews in the world aren't sitting together right this minute. That's what you would logically expect, because the Bible calls us 'one people on earth.' It's only our sins that have made us lose our sense of oneness, lose it completely! May a merciful God bring us together again and may we soon see the day on which we worship him with one heart. *L'hayyim*, Jews, *l'hayyim!*"

Nachum Berish sighed again and said:

"As for the cause of the matter—that is, the matter of the cause—of unity and disunity, I've completed a great inquiry into it that I had intended to give as a sermon on the Sabbath before last Yom Kippur. I'm sure that had I given it, I would have been told it was sweeter than honey."

"Who needs inquiries?" asked Alter Lipa. "I'm against them. Even if they're begun for good reasons, they end in heresy and disbelief. Look at the generations before the Flood. They were great inquirers. They asked questions about everything, and in the end—piff, paff, poof, look what became of them! Only why go back to the Flood? I remember an incident in our town in Galicia. There was a young man who was supported after his wedding by his father-in-law, wined and dined by him in style. Since he didn't have to work, he began to read books of philosophy until he became a philosopher himself, and wanted to know all the answers, and nearly went out of his mind. If he hadn't been brought to Rabbi Hanoch of Elsk, may his righteousness protect us, who brought him back to his senses, he would have taken leave of them completely. *L'hayyim*, Jews, *l'hayyim*! God save us from all philosophy. May we worship Him in simplicity as befits the descendants of Jacob, whom the Bible calls a simple man."

"If you have a bone to pick with your rabbi," Kitzingen said, "I'll ask you to do it in your synagogue. Don't waste the time of a businessman like me who has to make a living. I didn't come here for empty talk."

"Sha sha sha!" Alter Lipa answered him. "What's all the fuss about? You call a Jewish conversation empty talk? Why, a Jewish conversation is holy. The Lord himself likes to listen in on one, and even the angels are jealous, since they can only talk by flapping their wings while Jews use their holy mouths. And as for making a living, I'm surprised you don't know that you can make a hundred million quadzillion times more money by talking, provided it's about the right thing. I'll give you a personal example. Once I was sitting with my rabbi in Galicia, may he live. He was in high spirits and he said, 'Lipa Alter'—that's what he called me, Lipa Alter, and I'm sure there's a great mystery in that—'Lipa Alter, ask whatever you want of me and it's yours. Just don't think before asking; say the first thing to cross your mind.' 'Rebbe,' I said to him, 'I'd like a silver snuff box.' Before I knew it he had a silver snuff box in his hand and it was mine. To think that I could have asked him for as many gold coins as there were grains of tobacco in that box and been as rich as Rothschild! That's what I mean by saying the right thing. *L'hayyim*, Jews, *l'hayyim*! Yudl, I see a plate of onion pletzels. Whew, they're peppery! How did they get here? I don't remember seeing them before. It must be our visitor who brought them. The rabbis knew what they were talking about when they said that whoever God sends into this world, he sends with a gift. *L'hayyim*, Jews, *l'hayyim*! May it be God's will that… that…."

Kitzingen stood up and said, "Herr Bieder, it's either the brandy bottle or our business. We can't have both. Save your stories for the

Hasidim in your synagogue, Herr Elbert. I didn't come here tonight to listen to them."

"Get a load of him!" mocked Alter Lipa. "You tell me, O wisest of Germans: What made you come in the first place? Was it your own idea? Whose brain told your feet to put on their fancy shoes and get themselves over here? If not for me, they wouldn't have bothered. And how did I do it if not with my stories? Do I have to remind you that we were sitting and talking about Dr. Levi's quarrel with the Reverend Gesetztreu? From there we got around to Levi's library, and someone said there might be money to be made from it. I cottoned to the idea, and I went and sussed out the market, and I nosed around here and there, and I heard all kinds of things about Levi's books, and I came to you and said, ay ay ay, we've hit the jackpot, let's go partners and bring in Rabbi Nachum Berish, he's a bit of a scholar and knows a thing or two about books. You tell me: is that how it was or isn't it?"

"To tell the truth," Nachum Berish said, "I'm not so sure how valuable Levi's library is. Men like him go in for all kinds of books that aren't worth very much. I can vouch for that from my own experience. Once a rich Jew in our synagogue was accused of dealing in contraband goods. He could have gone to prison for years, God save us, and so he came to me and said, 'Rabbi, pray for me.' I prayed for his acquittal and my prayers were granted. He wanted to thank me, so he went to a neighbor of his, a fellow named König, who said to him, 'If you want to give your rabbi a nice present, buy him a biblical cyclepedia.' He took a wad of money and bought a cyclepedia and brought it to me pleased as punch, as if he were giving me, ay ay ay, who knows what treasure. If you ask me, the only difference between a cyclepedia and any other old book is that most old books lose their bindings and this cyclepedia was bound in leather with gold letters."

"You've told me our friend here was an acquaintance of Dr. Levi's and knows what books he had," Kitzingen said. "Since he's turned up tonight, let's ask him what he thinks of the transaction. Any way you look at it, there isn't much of a market for books."

"Who needs a market?" asked Alter Lipa. "On the contrary! If there's no market, we'll buy them on the cheap. We'll leave the selling of them to God, who sees to it that Jews make a living. The main thing is to get our hands on them before anyone else does. Once they're ours, ay ay ay, we can do what we want with them. But just look at all of you, sitting around this table as if there were nothing on it. Pour yourselves a drink and let's toast our heaven-sent guest. *L'hayyim*, gentlemen, *l'hayyim!*"

"I can see you've made up your minds to take him in as a fourth partner," Kitzingen said. "Far be it from me to object to one more Jew making some money on my account. But we've wasted enough time. The reason I was against brandy is that drink leads to empty talk and empty talk doesn't go with doing business."

"To listen to you," said Alter Lipa, "a person might think that brandy wasn't a business. I know lots of good Jews who grew rich from selling brandy and are such millionaires today that by comparison all the businessmen of Leipzig are like a rat's tail to a Hasid's fur hat. Besides which, more than one business deal has been made over a glass of brandy. On the contrary! Nachum Berish can tell you that the two jugs of brandy he donated to a celebration in our synagogue are what made him its rabbi. There's no need to be embarrassed, Nachum Berish: brandy is a kosher drink and many a kosher Jew owes his life to it. You, too, Kitzingen, to call you by that German name of yours. If some matchmaker hadn't drunk too much brandy, he would never have talked your rich wife into marrying you. And if you have any complaints about her, we have a rabbi right here. He'll be glad to arrange a divorce."

"I won't be talked to like that!" shouted Kitzingen, banging the table.

"It seems our German has a temper," mocked Alter Lipa. "He doesn't like the way I talk! Don't you know that the angels in heaven rack their brains over every word a Jew utters because there's nothing as deep as Jewish talk? Why, half a sentence, spoken by a Jew, has more wisdom in it than all the books of philosophy since Aristotle—provided, of course, that the Jew keeps away from falsehood and the Evil Tongue."

"Either you shut up," Kitzingen said, "or you can count me out of this deal."

"If you're out, we're still in," said Alter Lipa.

"With whose money?" Yudl asked.

"Money, money, money!" Alter Lipa exclaimed. "That's all some people can think about."

"If you're so smart," Yudl said, "let's see you do business without it."

"Look at what happened in my hometown in Galicia," said Alter Lipa. "There was a water carrier there, the poorest of the poor, he didn't even own his own buckets—and one day he won the state lottery without putting out a penny. Do you think it was a miracle? It was simplicity itself! It's just that compared to such simplicity, the wildest stories you've heard are like a fingerbowl set beside the sea."

Kitzingen took out his watch and said:

"At exactly eleven o'clock I'm leaving you and your wild stories and going home."

"Ay ay ay!" Alter Lipa said. "Back in Galicia, we'd pawn a watch like that and buy ourselves a jug of honey schnapps. Have any of you gentlemen noticed that you can't find a drop of honey schnapps in all of Germany?"

"That's not the only thing you can't find in Germany," said Nachum Berish. "It beats me why God goes out of his way to help the Germans win their wars. Jewish learning, there's none here; religion, none; Hasidism goes without saying. I suppose God must want Germany to conquer the Russian Empire so that Russian Jews can teach German Jews Torah. But if all the best Jews in Russia come to Germany, what will be left of Jewish life there?"

"It will be like Lithuania," said Alter Lipa, "in which you can't find a Hasid for love or money."

Kitzingen rose to his feet. "Good night, gentlemen," he said.

"Where are you rushing off to?" asked Yudl Bieder. "Now that we've been joined by our friend who has seen Dr. Levi's books and visited his widow, let's hear what he has to say." With a glance at me Yudl said, "You must have realized by now that we're thinking of buying Levi's library. What's your opinion? Is it a good investment?"

"Good or not," said Alter Lipa, "it's not the investment that counts, it's God's blessing. What, you're leaving us too? Before you do, there's something I wanted to ask you. This Dr. Mittel of yours—isn't he from a family of Kotsk Hasidim? In Galicia we say, there's no greater misfortune for Hasidism than a Kotz Hasid. I've heard that you and Mittel are thick as thieves. In that case, please tell him for me, 'Herr Doktor,' tell him, 'don't be a Kotsker. Tell the judge that a Hasidic schmooze is a Hasidic schmooze and that there was no oath or whiff of an oath. A Jew was schmoozing plain and simple, that's all there is to it.' Gentlemen, you know I'm a man of few words. But now I have to speak out, and you'll hear the truth whether you want to or not. If you're a Kotzk or Bratzlav Hasid, you're worse than no Hasid at all."

"You wicked, sinful man!" Yudl exclaimed, clutching his beard. "How dare you say such a thing? The Bratzlaver was the Baal Shem Tov's great-grandson, a pure and holy Jew."

"I suppose," said Alter Lipa, "that the Zionists are pure and holy, too, because they're descended from Abraham, Isaac, and Jacob. Did Abraham, Isaac, and Jacob try buying the land of Israel from the Turks? That's what the Zionists proposed to do, and make us live there with them to boot. Thank God we have the choice to let them live there by themselves. And if you think the anti-Zionists are any better, I tell you it's one big Pharaoh's dream. Politics, gentlemen, started before the Flood when politicians built the Tower of Babel. One said, 'Give me water to make bricks,' so another passed him a bucket of dirt; this man asked for a crowbar and that one handed him a rake. In the end, they beat each other's brains out. Rabbi Nachum Berish, you tell us: Isn't that what happened? Doesn't it say so in our holy books? But look here: you're all sitting around a table with a bottle of brandy on it as though you were in mourning for the Temple! *L'hayyim*, Jews, *l'hayyim!*"

Chapter fifteen

The next morning I tried phoning Lunenfeld again, once more without success. The hotel manager took the receiver from me and shouted at the operator:

"What's going on, are you fast asleep?"

Before the operator could answer, a woman in a nurse's uniform came down for her breakfast. When she saw me she rose from her table, held out her hand, and said with a smile:

"I hope your luggage arrived safely."

Realizing she was Sister Bernhardina, I assured her that I would have recognized her anywhere, in uniform or out. We conversed for a while and I told her I had been trying to get through to Lunenfeld for the past twenty-four hours. Bernhardina looked at the number I was dialing and said:

"You copied it wrong. This isn't our number. I'll put you through to the nursing home at once."

"First," I said, "let's finish our conversation."

I put a few more questions to her and she answered them. In the end, she said:

"Why bother telephoning? Come with me to Lunenfeld and you can return to Leipzig with Frau Schimmermann tomorrow."

"Is she planning to be in Leipzig tomorrow?" I asked.

"Tomorrow," Bernhardina said, "Professor Nadelsticher from Berlin is giving a lecture at the Leipzig Evangelical Society and Frau Schimmermann promised our doctor's wife to go with her."

I asked, without mentioning Nadelsticher's hat:

"Is your doctor's wife such a great lecture-goer, then, that she insists on traveling to Leipzig to hear Nadelsticher?"

"Don't you know she's his daughter?" asked Bernhardina.

"She is?"

"I thought you knew. She told me she remembered you from her parents' home and asked me to let her know the next time you're in Lunenfeld. She's been writing poetry and has a batch of poems she'd like to show you. Ach, *mein Herr*, when you read them you'll see how noble a German woman's heart is! I simply don't understand why the newspapers refuse to print them. They're no different from all the other patriotic poems that you see in them all the time."

"To tell you the truth," I said to Bernhardina, "I'd travel to Lunenfeld just for those poems if only I weren't in a hurry to get back to Berlin. And now that I've found someone to convey my best wishes to Frau Schimmermann, there's no need for me to phone."

As I was leaving the hotel, Herr Kitzingen passed by with Alter Lipa on his heels. As soon as he saw me, Alter Lipa abandoned Kitzingen's company for mine. Hooking his walking stick over his arm, he rubbed his hands with satisfaction and said, "It's a pleasure to step out and run into a fellow Jew! And not just a Jew, but a good friend, closer to me than a brother. I hadn't hoped to see you again so soon, because Yudl Bieder told me you were just passing through. The best treat is an unexpected one! I don't want to detain you, so I'll walk you wherever you're going, even to Mittel's house, although only as far as his front door. You mustn't think, God forbid, that I bear Mittel a grudge. On the contrary, I love the man dearly. If he had a chicken to slaughter, I'd do it for free. And if he dislikes me, that has nothing to do with me personally, God forbid. It's because

I'm a Galician Hasid and he dislikes us all equally. I don't have to tell you what fine people we Galician Hasidim really are. If all other Jews were like us, the Messiah would have come long ago. Not that Mittel should surprise one. Aren't we told that when the Temple stood in Jerusalem, with its high priests and sacrifices and Sanhedrin and great saints all serving the Lord in perfect righteousness, the city was full of feuds and quarrels? So what can you expect of a Christian city like Leipzig, in which there are hardly any Jews and most of them are worse than Christians? But I shouldn't be so hard on Jews when the times are hard enough on them. As long as I've mentioned Mittel, who's now the legal expert on everything I say, let me tell you a story. Once there was a righteous Jew who was accused of a crime he didn't commit. By chance, the judge at his trial happened to be Jewish too, though only in the flimsiest way. When the trial was over, the Jew was acquitted. This aroused his envy: since there is no greater good deed than defending the righteous from injustice, why should a freethinker like the judge get the credit for it? And so he waited for him outside the courtroom and proposed when he came out, 'Sell me your good deed and I'll give you a yarmulke full of gold coins.' The judge refused. Some other Jews were standing nearby. 'Just look at what a good deed can do!' the righteous Jew said to them. 'It can make a Jewish judge in a Christian court so wise that he won't trade it for a yarmulke of gold coins.' The next time you see Mittel, you might pass that on to him. Let him know the only reason God made him a witness at my trial is to get credit for helping a Jew in distress."

I had barely parted from Alter Lipa when I bumped into an antiques dealer I knew. He had heard I was the executor of Dr. Levi's library and wanted to know what was in it. Not wanting to spend another night in Leipzig and run up more hotel bills, I cut short the conversation.

Back at the hotel, I was told that a gentleman had left a letter for me. I wondered who it might be. It wasn't Yudl Bieder, because no Christian in Leipzig would call a Galician Jew a gentleman behind his back. It wasn't König, because even if he had heard that I'd been to the foundry, he had no way of knowing what hotel I was at. And for the same reason, it couldn't be Dr. Mittel. Could it be Gerhard Schimmermann with a message from Brigitta, who had heard about me from Bernhardina?

I opened the letter and saw that it was from Hirsmann the bookstore owner, who had looked for me at the hotel and would be grateful if I'd come to his store. Clearly, he too was interested in Levi's books and hoped to pump me for information. Alas, I wasn't what the rumors, which I could only think of as some sort of punishment, made me out to be. I paid my bill at the hotel, took my bag, went to the train station, and bought a ticket for Berlin.

And so once again I stood in the large station with trains coming and going all around me. While I was waiting for the train to Berlin, the Grimma train pulled in on the next track. For a moment, I considered traveling to Grimma in the hope of talking Dr. Levi's widow out of selling his books. While God is my witness that I've always minded my own business, especially in financial matters, I felt an obligation to thwart the plan that Alter Lipa Elbert, Nachum Berish, Yudl Bieder, and Kitzingen were hatching. You mustn't think I had anything against them. Yudl Bieder's apartment was a second home to me in all the years I lived in Leipzig. And in any case, go do something rash when the German police keep track of all your movements! As my permit was only for a Berlin-Leipzig round-trip, an excursion to Grimma was out of the question.

God would do with Levi's books as he saw fit, I thought, leaving their fate to Providence. I had done what I could. I boarded the train for Berlin, in which there was barely room to stand, made myself as small as I could, and bounced up and down and off the other passengers. In keeping with their size and the vicissitudes of the train's progress, they bounced back at me.

Once more, as on the night trip with Brigitta's troops, I was returning to Berlin. Then, though, I was worried about finding a room, whereas now I had one waiting for me, nicely furnished and laid-out, even if its landlady was a hard woman.

I don't wish to make my room sound better or my landlady worse than they were. I'll only say that it's sometimes worth putting up with a hard landlady in order to have a nice room. In a lighter vein I might observe that, if three things are needed for a man's peace of mind, the right woman, the right room, and the right furnishings, any combination of two should be enough for a temporary boarder.

The train's compartments were full and the air grew steadily more foul. Like most of the passengers, I chain-smoked to keep it at bay. Each time I lit another cigarette I wondered whether, had he been in my place, the grocer from Grimma could have resisted the temptation of smoking the three cigars he kept in his jacket pocket for the day his sons returned from the war. Just as I lit my last match and smoked my last cigarette, the black pall of Berlin loomed on the horizon.

We arrived in the city at nightfall. I had a bite to eat and took the underground to Friedenau. I left the lights off when I entered my room. My eyes were smarting from the long day and it felt good to let them rest.

I sat thinking of my trip to Leipzig. Had it been worth the expense and aggravation just to bring Nadelsticher his hat? As hard as I thought about it, I could get no further than this: if a man's every task from birth to death is decreed in advance, whatever isn't finished must be returned to—and if isn't finished the second time, there'll be a third and a fourth and as many times as it takes. Although I had no idea what I still had to do in Leipzig, there was now one less trip to make before setting out for Palestine.

After sitting for a while, I rose and took a few steps. The floor-boards creaked beneath me. I walked back the other way and they creaked again. Turning on the light, I saw that the carpet was gone and that my room had been oddly transformed. Its furnishings had vanished, their place taken by hideous junk. Apart from the wood-cuts from the *Nibelunglied*, there was nothing left for me to take the slightest pleasure in.

I paced back and forth, the floorboards groaning furiously with each step. Likewise, the knight Hagen. Although I can't say he had begun to speak from the wall, his angry stare spoke for itself. His thin, bony face, its melancholy eyes reminiscent of Papa Wrangel's, as Berliners called the nineteenth-century field marshal, was hard and cruel with a touch of something else—something midway between despair and bottomless lust. As long as my room had boasted of its furnishings, I hadn't noticed this about him. Now that they were gone, Hagen was showing his true colors.

I called for the landlady. She didn't come. I went to look for her in the kitchen and found her sitting with a pack of puppies and smooching with one of them, her lips puckered for it to lick off their spittle.

"Good evening, *meine Frau*," I said. "What have you done to my room?"

"What have I done to your room?" she asked, straightening up with the puppy in her arms and standing as tall as her little figure allowed, teeth bared. "What have *I* done to your room?"

I said, "You haven't done anything, of course. You've simply taken away all its furnishings."

She began to swear a blue streak at the carpenter, who had come with the police and removed her son's things.

"What you've put in their place couldn't be uglier," I said.

"Don't talk to me about ugliness," she said. "It isn't ugly to shyster a woman whose son has fallen for the Fatherland?"

The shyster, so it seemed, was now me. This isn't the time or the place to relate our conversation or to repeat every one of the names she called her husband when he came to my defense. "French frog" was one of them. "Judas Iscariot" was another. "Rotten limey" was a third.

I realized that it was pointless to go on living there and that I had better look for another room. The whole rigmarole began all over again. And when at last I found a place, there was no one to move me, because anyone whose two arms hadn't been lost in the war wanted a fortune for the use of them. If it hadn't been for Peter Temper, who sent me an employee of the zoo's known as Der Schöner Buliml, all my belongings would have remained with the dog-lady. Even then she kept some of them, filching a few things that she fancied. None of it mattered to me very much except for a linen sheet that my mother, may she rest in peace, had given me when I left home for Palestine. According to Der Schöner Buliml, he saw the dog-lady remove it from a carton and said to her, "That belongs to the gentleman." "If it did, I wouldn't take it," she said. "I say it does," he said. "And I say it doesn't," she said. "I'm going to tell him," said Der Schöner Buliml. "Tell him what you want," said the dog-lady. "I will," he said. "I wouldn't if I were you," she said, "because then he'll accuse you of stealing it."

Just then her husband came along and demanded to know what was happening. Told by Der Schöner Buliml, he said to his wife, "Bitch, give him his sheet or I'll crack your skull in two!" They began to fight and Der Schöner Buliml made his getaway. Although he must have assumed I would get my sheet back, I never did. I didn't return to ask for it afterwards either, because I was occupied with my new room.

I only call it a room because in those days anything could pass for one. Apparently, the dog-lady's room had been spreading gossip about me and my new room's walls heard it and passed it on to the chambermaid. The chambermaid relayed it to the landlady, and the landlady began to treat me like a disreputable character. Before long the chambermaid realized that she could get away with anything. She stole from me and behaved rudely on purpose, so that if I called her a thief she could say I was just getting back at her. But though I should have looked for another room, I didn't bother to. By now I knew from experience that every room was worse than the one before. As far as I could see, there was a grand conspiracy of rooms against me. This took the form of a syndicate. If any member of it was told, "You bad room, you, how can you be so mean to a perfectly decent tenant," it answered its accuser, "Very well, then, he's now yours. Let's see you do better." And while I'm hardly objective, I can assure you that none did. In the end, I fell ill from all my worries and had to go to the hospital. Telling you about that would involve writing another book. The one good thing was that I didn't have to report to the draft board as long as I was hospitalized.

At this point, I might also tell you how I finally bought new clothes and new shoes when everything in my closet began to fall apart. However, as I don't wish to be blamed for the crassness of going on a wartime shopping spree, I'll skip the details. This will also save me the trouble of explaining that I didn't buy the right things, because they were summer items on sale and it was now a cold, snowy winter.

I'll get back to my room. I lived a joyless, thankless existence in it, regularly paying an exorbitant rent for which I was billed by my landlady in elegant columns of figures. Germany had every reason to be proud of its school system: not only could ordinary women who were forced to take in boarders read, write, and do sums, many knew half of Schiller's poems by heart and could declaim them with great passion. The national poet was so good at getting the female sex to quote him on art, justice, and integrity that it thought that Germany alone, of all the countries in the world, possessed such things. And yet no sooner did your German hausfrau have a chance to jack up prices than all of Schiller's odes went by the wayside.

And so I lived where I lived, nodding wearily at every injury and insult, sometimes laughing through my tears and sometimes leaving out the laughter. Once, for instance, my landlady billed me for half a lemon, even though I hadn't seen a lemon since the war broke out. "What is this half-lemon you're charging me for?" I asked her.

"There was a stain on your tablecloth," she replied. "The only thing that took it out was lemon juice."

"Speaking of my tablecloth," I said, "where is it?"

"It tore in the wash and had to be thrown out," she explained.

"You're a formidable person, Frau Blutwarm," I told her. "There's not a lemon peel to be found in all of Germany, yet you used half a lemon to clean a tablecloth."

Frau Blutwarm acknowledged my praise with the demure smile of German womanhood.

In this way a month went by, and another and another, and every Monday and Thursday I reported to the draft board to have my heart checked for its military value. As it was not in the best of shapes, the generals hadn't wanted it. Yet as the war dragged on and the cream of German youth was led to the slaughter, the generals grew less choosy. It came to the point that just standing on your two feet was enough to pass the medical.

One day I traveled to Tempelhof with the other cases. Some were disfigured, some covered with sores, some half-blind or half-lame, some afflicted with every imaginable illness. I looked at all that living flotsam being towed to the parade grounds and I thought, I may have kept out of the war so far, but from now on I'd be in trouble even if I were a good Jew-hating German and not an Austrian-Jewish draft dodger. Adding my own debris to the wreckage, I reported to Tempelhof. We were taken to a yard where officers sat at tables and decided whom to send to the front at once and whom to save for the next time. As long as the men had their clothes on, they looked halfway human. Once they undressed, they resembled corpses awaiting their burial. I put my trust in the God of All Souls and began taking off my shoes and shirt before joining the line.

All around me men were whispering. I listened and heard someone say that the German fleet had mutinied. Although it wasn't clear what was happening, it was obvious that something had changed. There was talk of revolution. Some said it had even begun. Before I could be marched off to the trenches, His Majesty the Kaiser fled Germany with his general staff. With no one left to make war, the war ended.

Were I to tell you everything that followed, the number of chapters, subchapters, and sub-subchapters in my story would be infinite. Some day, if God gives me strength and ink, I'll perhaps write a thousandth part of the thousandth part of it. In this particular book, I've sought to relate one sequence of events from the time of the war. I'm not one for grand notions and I prefer to deal with small things. Still, there's no denying that small things add up to big ones. Because I couldn't find a room in Germany, I had the good fortune to return to Palestine. God give me strength and a last drop of ink and I'll tell you about that now.

The thought of returning to Palestine made me so happy that I put everyone out of my mind: my friend Peter Temper and his zoo with its big cats, and the eminent bibliographer Dr. Mittel, and the charming Brigitta, and everyone else whose friendship I had valued while living in Germany—to say nothing of Dr. Levi's widow, whom I had stopped thinking about on the day I heard she was incurably ill.

But this same woman, of whose life all had despaired, recovered miraculously. Indeed, not only did she return to her old self, she was more vital than ever and healthier than any of her doctors, including the young physician on duty the day I visited her in the hospital. Of course, I'm exaggerating a bit. In reality, there's no need to invoke miracles in an age in which they no longer occur. What happened was this. One day Frau Levi felt that her bandages were pressing on her and asked the doctors to loosen them. "That's impossible," they said, alarmed by her request, as she would be in grave danger if the bandages weren't airtight. Not only weren't they loosened, they were tightened even more until she felt she couldn't breathe. As soon as no one was looking, she stuck a finger inside them and wriggled it to make some room. At once she felt better. Gradually, she worked off all her bandages. As soon as they were loose her strength returned to her. She sat up, opened her eyes, and saw she was lying in a hospital bed piled with pillows and blankets, screened off from the other patients, and surrounded by a stack of medicines so high that it shut out the sunlight. She tried pushing the medicines away—and even as her white-robed attendants stood whispering that her end was near, she realized she could move her arm. Next, she stood up. Then she ordered the attendants to bring her clothes. No one dared disobey her. When she was fully dressed, her color returned and she walked out of the hospital and back to her old life.

Where was I? Unable to find a room in Germany, I was obliged to return to Palestine. And since Palestine, too, was in shambles from the war and not everyone could find a room there either, I bought some land and built a house with several rooms. Not that I needed more than one room for myself, but I also needed space for Dr. Levi's library. Shortly before setting out, I received a letter from his widow informing me of her plans to settle in Palestine herself and of her quandary concerning her husband's books. Taking all of them with her was more than she could manage, while choosing some and leaving others meant playing favorites with a collection that her husband had loved in its entirety. It was then that it occurred to me that, by adding more rooms, I could accommodate all of Levi's books.

Before I knew it, my house was finished. That's one of the good things about Palestine: as its builders wish to see it rebuilt, they work quickly and meet all their deadlines. As soon as I was able to move in, I took one room for myself and set aside the others for Dr. Levi's books, of which I can only say that the more I think of them, the more precious they become to me and the more I think of myself. When I stroll through the empty rooms that soon will hold them, I'm moved to speak in praise of all things that turn out for the best. Consider what happened to a man like me. Living in cramped quarters without pleasure or sunlight, he received a letter from Dr. Levi's widow asking to consult with him about her husband's books; traveling to see her, he found her hopelessly ill; returning to Berlin in frustration, he had nowhere to lay his head, his room having been given to another; finding another room that he liked, he was soon driven from it and forced to wander from place to place, from room to room, and from tribulation to tribulation, his worries multiplying without cease. And yet just when it seemed that he could no longer bear one more of them, God had mercy and delivered him and returned him to the Land of Israel. Is not all that seems for the worst, then, really for the best? And the best of all I've saved for last, which is the house this man built in Palestine. Not being one for grand notions, he knows that he built it not for himself but for Dr. Levi's books, which needed a new home.

And because so many things befell me and I lived to tell about them all, I have called this book "To This Day" in the language of thanksgiving for the past and of prayer for the future. As it says in the Sabbath morning service: To this day have thy mercies availed us and thy kindness not failed us, O Lord our God. And mayst thou never abandon us ever.

About the Author

S.Y. Agnon was born Shmuel Yosef Halevi Czaczkes in Buczacz, Eastern Galicia. In 1908 he immigrated to Ottoman Palestine, there to publish his first story, *"Agunot,"* ("Forsaken Wives"), under the pen name "Agnon"—a surname he later adopted legally. After an extended stay in Germany from 1913 to 1924, he returned to Jerusalem, where he remained until his death in 1970.

Called "a man of unquestionable genius" and "one of the great storytellers of our time," S.Y. Agnon is among the most effusively praised and widely translated of Hebrew authors. Extolled for the uniqueness of his style and the beauty of his language, as well as his comic mastery, Agnon's contribution to the renewal of Hebrew literature has been seminal for all subsequent Israeli writing. While much of his work attempts to recapture the lives and traditions of a former time, his stories are never a simple act of preservation, bur rather deal with the most important psychological and philosophical problems of his generation, touching on the spiritual desolation of a world standing on the threshold of a new age.

The winner of numerous Israeli prizes (Bialik Prize, 1934 and 1950; Israel Prize, 1954 and 1958), Agnon was awarded the Noble Prize for Literature in 1966.

The fonts used in this book are from the Garamond family

The Toby Press publishes fine writing,
available at leading bookstores everywhere. For more
information, please visit www.tobypress.com